OUT OF TIME

OUT OF TIME

Louise Pakeman

CHIVERS
THORNDIKE

This Large Print book is published by BBC Audiobooks Ltd, Bath, England and by Thorndike Press®, Waterville, Maine, USA.

Published in 2005 in the U.K. by arrangement with Saltwater Press.

Published in 2005 in the U.S. by arrangement with Saltwater Press.

U.K. Hardcover ISBN 1–4056–3443–X (Chivers Large Print)
U.S. Softcover   ISBN 0–7862–7900–1 (British Favorites)

The text of this Large Print edition is unabridged.
Other aspects of the book may vary from the original edition.

Set in 16 pt. New Times Roman.

Printed in Great Britain on acid-free paper.

British Library Cataloguing in Publication Data available

Library of Congress Cataloging-in-Publication Data

Pakeman, Louise, 1936–
       Out of time / by Louise Pakeman.
            p.   cm.
       "Thorndike Press large print British favorites."—T.p. verso.
       ISBN 0–7862–7900–1 (lg. print : sc : alk. paper)
       1. Real estate agents—Fiction. 2. Large type books. I. Title.
PR9619.4.P35O96 2005
823'.92—dc22   2005013644

For Mike

CHAPTER ONE

'You haven't changed,' he said softly, his forefinger under her chin tilting her face upwards so that she had no choice but to look directly into his eyes.

They stood for a moment, quite still as if frozen in time, cocooned by the silence and linked by the intimacy of the gesture. For a second, or eternity, Fern met his gaze before dropping her eyes.

Mutual embarrassment replaced the strange spell before he dropped his hand abruptly and, as if on cue, they moved apart. The intense emotion engendered was isolated in a brief capsule of time as if it had never been. Fern might have succeeded in obliterating it entirely, but for the still present touch of his finger on her skin.

Paul shrugged and held both hands palm up, an expressive Gallic gesture unusual in an Australian. There was a comforting familiarity about it, which was odd, for until about half an hour ago, her only contact with this man had been a short telephone conversation to arrange this meeting in his office.

She wondered why she hadn't queried his odd remark, and simply walked out, then and there. She had just stood there, gazing into his eyes, like a lovesick schoolgirl. She cringed

1

with embarrassment.

'As you don't seem to have anything suitable to rent I had better look at properties you have for sale.' Her voice was cool to the point of being glacial as she attempted to dismiss the uncomfortable moment and get back on a business footing with this odd stranger.

'Of course . . .' he mumbled, rattling his car keys in his hand as he moved to the door.

As she preceded him into the street, Fern wasn't sure whether she was more annoyed with him for his idiotic gesture or herself for her response. It was not part of her self concept to lose her cool when a man, however attractive, made a pass at her.

He watched her fold her long legs gracefully as she slid into the passenger seat of his car, caught a whiff of her perfume and admired the burnished copper of her sleek smooth bob.

He had always admired her hair . . . there he went again. It was crazy but she seemed as familiar to him as his own reflection in the mirror. That sudden snatch of perfume had triggered off some long buried memory. He was frowning slightly, in an effort to recall the place and circumstance of their last meeting, as he walked around to the driver's side. He needed to remember in order to give himself, if not her, a satisfactory explanation for his sentimental gesture when she first walked into his office.

They broke the uncomfortable silence

simultaneously.

'I am sure I have never met you before . . .' Fern's voice was deliberately distant, she wanted to let him know that she had no intention of being hooked by such stale bait as the *'don't I know you from somewhere else'* line. She pushed aside the fleeting recognition in that disturbing moment as their eyes met. Her lips set in a tight line as she added, 'Quite sure.'

He glanced at her sideways as he turned the key in the ignition; 'Well, I feel sure I have met you,' he insisted.

Involuntarily, Fern half turned toward him. As their eyes met she was aware of a strong undertow of attraction but quickly suppressed it. She neither knew, nor wanted to know him.

Her purpose in coming here was to forget, not remember.

With a slight shrug she forced herself to turn away, muttering, 'You are very persistent,' as Paul released the handbrake and turned his attention to the road.

'Have you always lived in Victoria?' His question broke the silence.

'No,' she told him, adding, to soften an abruptness verging on rudeness, 'I was brought up in Tasmania.'

'I've never been there. I'm a New Zealander.'

'I visited relatives, in the North Island, near Wellington last year. Perhaps you saw me at

3

the airport, even on the plane.' She could acknowledge he had caught a glimpse of her somewhere.

'No,' he shook his head, 'I haven't been back for six years, and anyway I come from the South Island, way south, near Dunedin. We must have run into each other somewhere else. I am sure I have met you,' he persisted and in spite of her obvious reluctance to pursue the subject, suggested other places where they might have met, but further speculation only revealed the unlikelihood. There seemed few times when they had even been in the same state at the same time.

'Perhaps we stood in a lift together—or passed each other on escalators going in opposite directions.' Fern spoke dismissively. The conversation was getting too probing. The last thing she wanted was anything at all bordering on the personal in a relationship with any man at the moment, her wounds were still too raw, too new to withstand even the suggestion of scrutiny.

Yet perversely, when he shrugged, 'Perhaps, or maybe I was just imagining things,' Fern was disappointed and annoyed with both Paul and herself. If he thought *she* was making a pass he was way off beam. She resolved not to make any more attempts at polite conversation and she doubted whether she would buy the house they were going to see.

'Penny for them.' He broke into her

4

thoughts and made her wonder if she had sighed out loud.

His voice had a quizzical lilt that struck a familiar chord and forced her to remind herself there was nothing familiar about this man. This had been a favourite remark of her grandmother, the words brought her to mind, that was all.

'I don't think they are worth so much.' Her cool tone did not invite further conversation, she had no wish to step in the quicksands of that all-encompassing intimacy again. 'How far is this place?'

It turned out to be a disappointment, an ordinary suburban house. If she had to buy, she wanted something more individual.

'I'd rather have something smaller. I don't mind it being a bit—well—rough.' The house they had just viewed was freshly decorated, but in what, privately, Fern considered execrable taste.

'There is an old cottage in Hervey Street.' He sounded doubtful, as well he might for the place had been on his books now for nearly six months. Ever since the last owner had died in fact. Normally an estate sale like this went quickly, but in this instance both the heirs and the executors were agreed that they would extract the maximum price a reluctant market would yield. As a result the old house remained unsold, looking ever more unloved as the weeks grew into months.

5

'One of those properties real estate agents describe as a "renovator's dream" is it?' Fern asked dryly.

Paul flashed her a quick smile of appreciation, but, 'Absolutely!' was his only comment as he turned into a tree-lined residential street which boasted an eclectic mix of architectural styles, just about everything seen in Australia since convict settlement. He drew up outside an old brick house, rendered and painted with a yellow wash that glowed golden in the late afternoon sun. Fern, in spite of herself, felt the first real stirring of interest. Perhaps a renovator's dream was just what she needed.

She got out of the car and walked towards the little wicket gate at the side of the main drive gate. With the expertise of long practice, she flicked open the latch and lifted the gate slightly before pushing it open.

'You've been here before?'

'No,' she turned to him in surprise. 'Of course not.'

He shrugged. 'It took me about five minutes the first time I came to figure out that latch.' He followed her down the brick path towards the house, a small but solid example of a late nineteenth century urban tradesman's dwelling. A verandah ran along the front, edged with the original iron lace. The solid front door, flanked on either side by a tall sash window, had a fan light of mauvey pink glass.

Even looking at it from outside, Fern was pretty certain it was flannel flower glass, so called because of its pattern, and one of the earliest examples of coloured glass in Australia. She felt a tremor of excitement as he held open the door and stepped back for her to enter.

Inside, it was dark and cool, just short of dank. Their footsteps echoed on the bare boards; there was a smell of mice and must. There was no air conditioning and open fires the only form of heating, while an archaic and rusting wood stove appeared to be the sole cooking device.

Fern walked up the central hallway, paused halfway, then stretched her hands out to either side and placed them palm down on the clammy walls. It was as if the house was a living entity and she needed to make physical contact with it. With the cold brick of the old walls against the palms of her hands she felt an odd sensation, not unlike jet-lag, a remote dream-like feeling as if she no longer inhabited her own body. She had the most curious feeling that it was waiting for her to bring it back to life, as if it knew that she, of all people, could do just that. Abruptly she dropped her hands to her sides. She shivered involuntarily, then pulled herself together and continued her inspection of the house. She moved into the main bedroom, as a shaft of sunlight shone through the grimy window and settled on a cobweb hanging from the ceiling.

It was a total wreck, or a renovator's dream, according to your viewpoint. Nigel wouldn't have let her get beyond the front door. For a crazy moment, she wondered how she would explain her purchase to him, but it was for sale with immediate possession. Against all common sense and logic, Fern knew she would buy this house.

The sound of Paul clearing his throat brought her back to the present and the realisation that he was watching her, trying to gauge her reaction. She turned to face him, her features impassive. She had no intention of letting him see how the place was affecting her.

'The bathroom—and—er?'

'Toilet?' he supplied for her. 'I'm afraid they are outside.'

'*Both* of them?'

'The bathroom certainly. The toilet, well, depends what you call outside,' he assured her with a solemnity that she felt merely disguised amusement.

She followed him through the back door, down a couple of steps worn by countless feet, into a draughty, galvanised lean-to built onto the back of the house. The open door of a small box-like structure in the opposite corner revealed a splendid new toilet in a particularly lurid shade of green. Brand-new tiles surrounded it.

'New. Put in by the owner himself who felt he was getting too old for the trip down the garden path.'

'I don't see a bathroom.'

'Well that really is outside.' He led the way through a rickety door made of wooden trellis.

It would barely keep a cat out let alone a cat burglar, Fern reflected gloomily as she picked her way across the neglected backyard toward a long shed.

Paul opened a door at one end, next to a small window. Of the four panes two were frosted, one clear, the fourth plywood. All were equally filthy.

'Laundry cum bathroom!'

She stood in the doorway finding it hard to believe anyone had ever used the place. The laundry part was an old-fashioned double trough, a cast iron bath, small in length but deeper than normal, with claw feet, constituted the bathroom. It was so filthy she decided bathing had not been on the agenda for the previous owner. But in spite of the dirt, she recognised the tub as the sort of genuine article much sought after by the restorers of old houses. Linking the two was an old hot water 'copper'. Another genuine article. It would look good, she thought, with plants in it, nasturtiums perhaps—or red geraniums. And the bath could always be re-surfaced for rehousing in a new bathroom, *inside* the house.

She was about to say this until she

remembered that she should bargain, not allow the agent to think she was prepared to pay the asking price without a murmur.

'I am interested, but think the price is too high, it would probably be cheaper to bulldoze it than restore it.'

'Probably,' Paul agreed, surprised that she appeared to be considering buying. 'Make an offer,' he suggested. Perhaps by now the vendors would be more reasonable.

She put forward a five thousand reduction on the asking price expecting it to be dismissed out of hand.

Tossing the keys from one palm to the other, a stab of conscience caused him to say, reluctantly, 'Maybe you had better look through again before you decide, discuss it with someone, your husband?' Paul wondered why he cared about her answer to this question. What difference did it make to him if the woman had a husband or not?

'This is my decision . . . my husband won't want anything to do with it.' Fern tagged the last bit on feeling she had responded too sharply to what, privately, she considered a chauvinistic remark. Now she wished she hadn't mentioned her husband, she might have to volunteer explanations at a later date. But what was it to him anyway? He was only selling her a house. Right now the problem was a suitable place to locate her new bathroom.

'Can you suggest someone to do the

necessary renovations?' she asked as they stood in the main bedroom staring at wallpaper, probably hung when the house was built, sagging from the wall.

'I can give you the name of a good man,' he promised, and silently admonished his wandering mind as he wondered why her husband would not be interested. Any man would certainly want everything to do with this woman!

'Thanks.'

She turned and walked out into the late afternoon sunshine. The garden, like the house, was a monument to neglect, but a hint of former glory was still discernible. It needed weeding and tidying up more than anything. She walked over to a lemon tree dropping ripe fruit onto the ground. She picked one up, tossing it in her hand, and turned to the overgrown roses blooming bravely in a circular, weed-filled bed. She plucked a half open bud and held it to her nose, savouring the delicate perfume with closed eyes. The sweet scent made her think of expensive toilet soap and at the same time transported her back to her childhood home in Tasmania. A rose very similar to this, maybe even the same variety, had tossed and smiled outside the bathroom window of the old farmhouse. She had reached to pick another bloom when she suddenly became aware that Paul had followed her out of the house and was watching her.

She turned towards him feeling guilty as she remembered that they didn't actually belong to her—yet.

'I am sure no-one will mind,' Paul reassured her, smiling. 'They won't know anyway, no-one ever comes here.'

'Who exactly are "they"?' Fern asked as they closed the wicket gate behind them. There was nothing about either the house or the garden that suggested anyone cared about them in the least. Her voice was sharper than she intended, reflecting the sudden surge of protective tenderness that she felt as she paused and looked back at the house and garden bathed in the mellow late afternoon sun.

'The Pommy owners who inherited the place.'

Her raised eyebrows invited more as she settled in the passenger seat.

'The old fellow lived by himself, it must be ten years since his wife died. About a year ago, the "do-gooders" moved in and got him into a "Home." He didn't last long after that.'

'You think they should have left him there?'

'I think we all have the right to live—and die—as we please.'

'I agree—to a point. But so often others get hurt in the process.'

He glanced sideways as she spoke and noticed her face had a closed, shuttered look.

'Not in this case,' he said dryly. 'His only son married an English girl who refuses to live in

Australia. They just want to sell and collect the cash. At least, that is what I understand from The Trustee Company who are the executors.'

'Well, looks like they may be lucky.'

'If they accept your price,' he reminded her. Privately he didn't think there was much doubt and wondered why he had been quixotic and suggested she make an offer.

'Your ad said, "two minutes from town centre", would that be correct—or real estate agent's time?' They had been driving for more than two minutes and they had not reached his office yet.

'As the crow flies.' Without looking at him she knew he was smiling.

In his office, he offered coffee and rummaged in his desk for the address he had promised her of a builder.

'You'll need to get some light in somehow. And of course redecorate throughout,' he mused as he stirred his coffee. He looked across his desk, wondering about her. He nearly suggested her husband might be able to do some of the work before remembering her distant reaction when he said something like that earlier.

'I think I know what to do with the interior once I have the structural work done, it is, after all, my metier.' She was perfectly polite but there was no mistaking the iciness in her voice. She drew a business card from her wallet and tossed it across the desk. 'You will

13

find my phone, fax, and e-mail details all there
. . . call me on my mobile when you get a
response from the vendors.'

Paul picked up the card and read the name
embossed on it:

Fern Barclay—Interior Designer.

The name rang a bell, perhaps someone had
told him about her, maybe he had read about
her in a magazine, even seen her picture. He
frowned, trying to remember. Pity he hadn't
known what she did before he started giving
her advice, obviously he had wounded her
professional pride.

'I shall be most interested to see what you
do with the old place,' he told her with an
apologetic smile and a slight shrug. If she
could make that dump look good, he would
take his hat off to her, he thought to himself.

Fern inclined her head slightly in
acknowledgement of his unspoken apology
then drained her coffee cup and got up to
leave. There was a powerful attraction about
this man, but she had no intention of
responding to it. 'The builder you were
suggesting . . .' she reminded him.

'Ahh—yes.' He passed her the business card
he had taken from his desk. 'I think you will
find him very satisfactory.' His voice matched
hers for coolness.

Fern tried to dismiss him as chauvinistic,
repressing the thought of his strange greeting
and the uncomfortable memory of her own

14

response. She reminded herself that she was her own person with an interesting and worthwhile career, and that she was starting over, without benefit of any man.

Yet, as she drove to the motel where she had stayed the previous night, she thought again about that odd greeting. Maybe he had, after all, really thought he knew her and was not just shooting a line.

Reluctantly, she acknowledged that there was a certain something about him, not the sort of person she would forget if he had ever crossed her path before.

Just a case of mistaken identity, she told herself firmly, slamming the doors of her mind, along with the car door, on the memory of the recognition that had flashed between them when he tilted her chin. She tried to convince herself that it had only existed in her imagination.

She had booked into the motel for two nights, not expecting to find anything she liked so quickly, if at all. Tired suddenly to the point of exhaustion, she was loath to eat in a public place. Crossing the road to a milk bar, she collected a simple takeaway meal—a salad roll, fruit juice and a bar of chocolate. She could add coffee and biscuits courtesy of the motel.

She had barely reached her room when her mobile phone began bleeping. It was Paul, her offer had been accepted.

Sitting in her room with her makeshift meal laid out in front of her, Fern felt a moment of panic as the realisation sank in that she had burned her boats, she had done it, bought a property. Hard on the heels of this thought chased another one. The place she had bought was not fit to live in, not by her standards anyway. If she tried to commute back and forth from Melbourne she would spend all her time on the road. The sensible thing would be to stay in Elmore while she got on with the renovating. But where? She would soon spend what money she had available at the motel, but as she had already tried to rent a place, she knew that was not going to be easy, or even possible. Never one to let the grass grow under her feet once she had decided on a course of action, she flipped Paul's card out of her wallet and dialled his mobile number. He promised to go through his rental listings again in the morning.

'Thanks. I will pay the deposit in the morning,' she told him. 'That is if you can find me a cheap place to live while I do up the cottage.' She had given herself an escape clause—strangely the thought did not give her any satisfaction.

She lay in bed walking through the house in her mind. It was a real challenge that would test her capability as an interior designer to the limit. For the first time in weeks, she was looking forward to the future with something like pleasure. Her last conscious thought before she fell asleep was that she must remember to take plenty of 'before renovations' photos, they would be of value to show up the 'after' ones she would take when the whole project was finished.

She dropped to sleep still mentally walking through the rooms of the old cottage, watching them change as she wove her artistry on them. Or endeavoured to, for she seemed to be discussing, or arguing with someone else about the pattern of the paper. She wanted a delicate sprigged flower pattern, soft and unobtrusive, the other—she was sure the shadowy 'other' was a man—was extolling the merits of a geometric pattern, very 'Art Nouveau' and not at all in keeping with the cottage.

She wondered, as she drifted into sleep, why Nigel was bothering about the wallpaper now he was dead, he never had when he was alive.

CHAPTER TWO

Stretching luxuriously in the strange but comfortable bed Fern tried, for a change, to recall the dream. She had been having such terrifying nightmares since Nigel's death that usually all she wanted to do was forget. But this was different, for once she had woken neither frightened nor angry, but intrigued. She remembered an argument about something, ah—yes—wallpaper. With some satisfaction she recalled that she had won and the main bedroom in the cottage had been papered with the old-fashioned floral paper. It had looked good. She resolved to search for one as similar as possible.

But who was she arguing with? Recalling the dream now she was fully awake she was sure it was not, as she had thought at the time, Nigel. Struggling to remember, it was the face of Paul Denton that she saw in her mind. This annoyed her. Attractive he may be, but he could keep out of her dreams. She dismissed the whole thing as nothing more than an extension of her waking preoccupation with the cottage. She sat up, stretched her arms, threw back the quilt and, swinging her legs over the side of the bed, walked over to the window.

Like her, the sleepy little town was waking to a new day. She did not regret her decision to stop here on her way north. Driving out of Melbourne, she had headed for the NSW border with the decision to stop when the fancy took her.

By the time she emerged from the shower, her breakfast tray had been delivered and a comforting smell of coffee and toast greeted her.

It was early when Fern arrived at Paul's

office, so early in fact that she wondered if he would be there. But she found him at his desk engrossed in the daily newspaper. He looked up when she came in and, although it was obvious that he had torn his eyes away from whatever it was he was reading, it was gratifying that his initial irritation changed to a pleased smile.

'You're an early bird!' He folded his paper as he spoke. Fern noted that it was the financial section, not the real estate that had absorbed him. Since success had put her into a higher income bracket, Fern had taken an interest in the stock market herself and would like to have sounded out his views, but he pushed the paper away now and opened a folder that lay underneath it. 'I have managed to find a flat that will be vacant in two weeks',' he told her. 'But I'm afraid it is very small, though within easy walking distance of the cottage.'

'I'll take it, it is only stopgap accommodation, so I don't mind it being small, especially if the rent is in the same league.' Then, remembering the real reason for her presence in his office, 'Or maybe I should settle for the cottage first?' Pulling out the chair opposite him, she drew her chequebook out of her bag and looked round for a biro. Ensuring that the cottage was truly hers was suddenly of prime importance.

'I wish all my clients were as easy to satisfy

19

as you,' Paul remarked some time later when they had settled all they could and Fern had handed over her deposit.

'Meaning?' She bridled at the touch of amusement in his voice.

He smiled openly as he replied, 'Well—you buy a house after a very cursory inspection and rent a flat without seeing it.' The rather deprecating shrug he gave left her in no doubt that he thought she was being precipitate—to say the least.

Fern stood up and looked him coldly in the eye. 'I should have thought it would be a pleasure to do business with someone who knows their own mind. As for the flat, well I have signed nothing on that, so you had better take me to see it.'

'Of course.' Ramming papers into his briefcase and snapping shut the clasp, he followed her to the door. God, but she was prickly!

It was, as he had warned her, small. Poky would have been her word, a bedroom with a corner marked off as a kitchen and a shared bathroom. 'I would call this a bedsitter,' she told him, but as she didn't intend to spend much time in it she added, 'It will do. I'll take it.' It was cheap, and very close to her cottage. With the deposit paid, she felt free to think of it as hers. The trustees were anxious to get things wound up and had agreed to a thirty day settlement. She would take the bedsitter for a

20

couple of months, and hope to have the cottage fit to live in by the end of that time.

'I shall have to go back to Melbourne to arrange to lease my unit there,' she explained to Paul. 'Having somewhere to stay will mean I can spend time up here and I thought . . . maybe if I could do something to the garden . . .' She trailed off leaving her words to explain themselves.

'I can't see that anyone is going to mind—or know,' he told her, the smile that touched his lips reflecting the surprising surge of pleasure he felt at the thought of her being in Elmore.

The warmth of his smile transformed his slightly sombre and rather craggy features. Fern felt her heart give an odd little 'blip' as she met his eyes and found she was smiling back. She turned quickly away and endeavoured to make her voice cool and businesslike as she quashed such errant thoughts. 'I shall have to go back to Melbourne later today, I'll contact your man about the renovations before I go. I'll bring gardening tools when I come back,' she added, more or less thinking aloud. 'I can't wait to tidy the garden up a bit, clear a few weeds, prune the roses, that sort of thing.'

'You like gardening?' Paul sounded surprised, he hadn't connected her with anything so earthy.

'Yes.' Reacting to the tone of his voice her reply sounded truculent. 'Do you?'

21

For a moment, she thought he was not going to reply. Then, 'I don't have a garden,' he said curtly.

A few moments ago he had appeared pleased that she would be living in the town—what had changed him? And what did she care either way. Her object in coming here had certainly not been to get involved with any man, even if he did make her heart go zing.

Heading back towards Melbourne, Fern slid a CD into the player and turned up the volume in a deliberate effort to erase all thoughts of Paul Denton and his strange greeting from her mind. She refused to think about her response and the magnetic attraction he had for her. The cottage was the only attraction for her in Elmore—her cottage—she reminded herself.

*   *   *

The next two weeks spent clearing up her affairs in Melbourne and arranging for the lease of her flat were so hectic that Fern did not have much time to brood. Although she did wonder from time to time what demon had driven her to take such drastic action. When she had first flung a suitcase in her car and driven north it had only been with the intention of stopping where the fancy took her and maybe renting accommodation for a few weeks to, as she told herself, 'get her life back on track'. How had she managed to commit herself to *buying* a property, and one that needed a complete make-over at that. Maybe, just maybe, that was just what she needed to re-build her own shattered self image.

In the busy-busy days of leasing her unit and packing up her belongings she managed to keep thoughts of Paul at bay, but as she left the city behind her she knew she was looking forward to seeing him again. She re-lived their meeting and wondered if they had met somewhere before. She couldn't dismiss it as a stupid pass on his part because she, too, had felt, if only briefly, that sharp stab of recognition. Besides she didn't think he was the sort of person to say a thing like that if he didn't think it true. She reminded herself that her decision to make this radical change in her life had nothing to do with Paul. But her foot dropped a little more heavily on the accelerator at the prospect of seeing him again.

Her nippy little hatchback, so good for city driving, was stuffed to the roof with those belongings she felt necessary for her well-being, even the front seat had her laptop computer lying by her hand-bag. It was occupying the space normally taken by Bubbles. For a moment the bulging car felt empty. Fern blinked and swallowed. Putting away her little friend's possessions, the tiny jewelled collar, the lead and waterproof coat, had been one of the sad parts of packing her life up and leaving the flat. She and Nigel had been so pleased when they found it, a ground floor one in a block of only six, in a quiet residential street only minutes from Central Melbourne. Most of their marriage had been spent there, it had seen the good times and the bad, the highs which, in the early days at least, had been peaks, and the lows which had seemed to get ever deeper.

Deciding that she was getting maudlin and failing to recall a hardware store in Elmore, Fern broke her journey in Castlemaine for a coffee and purchased a few basic gardening tools; a sturdy fork, a spade, a trowel, secateurs and a stout pair of gloves. Armed with these, she felt ready to do battle with the wilderness that would soon be hers.

She drove straight to Paul's office and felt a sharp stab of disappointment when he was not there and the girl at the reception desk handed her the key to her bedsitter. There she began the task of unloading the crammed car and re-stuffing her belongings into the small space.

By the time she had finished it was too late, and she was too tired, to do anything more than make herself a snack with the food she had brought with her and roll into bed. She switched off her mobile phone, if Paul hadn't contacted her by now, he didn't intend to. Why, anyway, should she expect him to? she asked herself, swallowing a sharp stab of disappointment along with a yawn.

She woke late after a mercifully dreamless sleep, eager to see her property and start work.

As Fern flicked up the latch on the front wicket she wondered why Paul had found it a problem. Slowly, she wandered around the small front garden then made her way out to the back. Surveying this overgrown and neglected wilderness, she had the curious feeling that it was waiting for her. This precious bit of land was her kingdom, to do with as she wished; she could nurture it and restore it or leave it just as it was. It gave her a feeling of empowerment yet at the same time she was overcome with a rush of almost maternal love for the tangled wasteland around her.

Common sense told her it would be foolish, if not pointless, to start on the part of the garden too close to the house, for when demolition of the appalling lean-to started, that area would probably be trampled. She decided to tackle the roses. It was not quite the right time of the year, buds were already opening on the tangled mass of brambles above the ground weeds. But she couldn't even get in to dig or weed with so much thorny growth.

She pulled on the new gardening gloves she had bought and, armed with her bright and, she hoped, sharp new secateurs went into battle. And battle it was; she was glad that she had had the sense to buy the strongest and best pair of secateurs in the shop but was soon wishing she had invested in a saw as well. After a while, she stopped worrying about making sure she pruned above an outward pointing bud, even above a bud, precepts about 'opening up the centre', and cutting out all the old wood were getting hazy as the morning progressed and the early September sun gained strength and warmth. As she scratched herself for the umpteenth time and a particularly long piece she was trying to throw to one side caught and grabbed her shirtsleeve and refused to be thrown, she decided it was time for a break. She collected her bottle of fruit juice from the car and collapsed on the cleanest, clearest bit of weedy grass she could find.

She leaned back with a sigh, feeling relaxed and almost happy. With the sun warm on her face, she felt her lids drooping, and lay back with closed eyes. Dispensing with sight, her other senses were assailed, the touch of the sun on her skin, the breath of a breeze, the smell of earth and the scents of the garden. She heard the distant hum of traffic, birds, a school bell clanging, the sharp barks of a dog in the street not far away.

Gradually the sounds faded to be replaced by the all too familiar ones from her recurring dream. The familiar voice with its command to look at the body in front of her, the details of the dream varied but in its essentials it was always the same.

This time it was on a makeshift stretcher, covered in some sort of rough sheet, she herself seemed to be standing on a balcony so that she looked down on the scene below. Commanding her attention as always was Nigel. The face was always unidentifiable, that was what made it so terrifying. This was when the guilt and fear became unbearable and she so often woke sweating and screaming. Then she heard another voice, a familiar man's voice, saying her name. First from a distance, then louder, closer.

She opened her eyes and for a moment was totally disorientated. The world had turned turtle. She was no longer standing looking down on—somebody. She was lying down while someone looked down on her.

'You?' was the only word she could find to say as she struggled to her feet, surprised and not a little relieved to find she was sensibly clad in jeans, not in the old-fashioned dress she had worn in her dream. 'What are you doing here?' Realising how ungracious she sounded, she added, 'I must have been dreaming.' She scrambled to her feet, brushing grass from her clothes to cover her embarrassment.

'I'm sorry, I didn't mean to alarm you. I happened to be driving past and when I saw your car I wondered how you were making out.' He looked around him as he spoke at the small patch of rose prunings and at the new fork still innocent of dirt.

'It doesn't look as if I have done much, but it is such a mess. I don't think anyone has touched this garden for years.' Fern was on the defensive. She couldn't think why; she had no need to justify herself to Paul.

'They haven't,' he agreed. 'Maybe you should get a gardener in to help?'

'No!' Hard work it may be, but she intended to do it herself. She had found the morning tiring, exhausting even, but therapeutic. 'I can manage. I am enjoying it,' she insisted.

Paul shrugged, took off his jacket, rolled up his sleeves and picked up the new fork. Without a word he began to turn over the weed-infested ground.

'You don't have to . . .' Fern protested somewhat half-heartedly.

'No, I don't,' he agreed.

Fifteen minutes later, Paul straightened up and surveyed the neat pile of weeds and turned up earth with satisfaction. He stuck the fork firmly in the ground and reached for his jacket.

'I must go now, but I enjoyed that, it cleared the cobwebs.' He flashed her a quick smile, and with the hand already raised in brief salute, brushed back his forelock, which was flopping forward after his exertion. He paused and looked at her. 'You'll be all right?'

'Of course,' she snapped, irritated that he

should ask and wondering why it had seemed so—normal to watch him working.

Paul shrugged, and turned away. He felt rebuffed, puzzled, and annoyed, in that order. Not one word of thanks for digging her damn garden. He ignored the fact that he had done it primarily for his own satisfaction. As he shrugged into his jacket he thought how vulnerable and appealing, and familiar, she seemed asleep. He had stood for a moment watching her, wondering where her dreams had taken her. For a crazy moment, he imagined she spoke his name.

Fern watched him leave, ruefully admitting that he had made more impression on the rose bed in fifteen minutes than she had all morning. She should have thanked him, she couldn't even remember saying 'goodbye'. She raised one hand in a half-hearted salute and opened her mouth to call a belated farewell, but even as she did so, she heard his car start. Perhaps it was as well, she had no wish to become emotionally involved, she reminded herself. Somehow the thought did not make her feel better. She decided to pack up her tools and call it a day.

That night for almost the first time in three months she slept a deep, dreamless sleep until the first fingers of dawn light stole into her bedroom. She woke refreshed and eager to tend her sad garden.

There was little she could do with the house

until settlement day when she became the legal owner in possession of the key, but she could work in the garden. The biggest event as the days passed was the increasing pile of weeds and rubbish. At night her bottle of sleeping tablets was left undisturbed in the bathroom, sheer physical exhaustion and the peace of mind that working in the old garden bestowed made them unnecessary.

There had been little peace in the ten years of her stormy roller coaster marriage to Nigel. At first the times of delirious joy had made up for the alternating, almost unbearable pain. Then the former had got less and the latter more and more frequent until the whole thing reached what she supposed was an inevitable conclusion.

'Never look back—Fern. The past is gone, don't waste time on it.' That had been Gran's good advice over so many things, but of course she did look back. Always wondering if she could have behaved differently and so altered the sequence of events. By picking up the shattered pieces of her life and making a determined effort to move forward, she was doing what Gran would have expected of her. And she would do it more effectively without the added complication of another man in her life. Holding that thought helped her to stop thinking about Paul.

She took a paperback novel with her now and read while she ate the salad roll and fruit juice she took for her lunch. She had no wish to be caught stretched out, asleep and dreaming again, but Paul didn't come and she wondered if he was deliberately keeping out of her way, and tried to be glad.

Fern was kneeling on the ground finally planting pansies around the edge of the now cleared rose bed when she became aware of being watched. She sat back on her heels and looked round, half hoping, in spite of herself, to see Paul. There was no-one there. Then, as she hooked out another plant from the punnet, she saw, out of the corner of her eye, a black and white cat sitting among the undergrowth in the untouched part of the garden. It was staring at her with a disconcerting intensity.

It wasn't that she disliked cats, quite the reverse. Memory, as it was apt to do, flooded her as she planted the last pansy. Selina, Gran's motherly old tabby, had been her closest friend for most of her childhood. But that was then, this was now and she did not want a cat in her garden or her life. 'Go away,' she shook her gardening gloves at it to reinforce her command.

It probably lived next door, she thought as it disappeared into the undergrowth against the wooden fence that divided her garden from the neighbour, and promptly forgot it, glad that she had achieved so much, for tomorrow was settlement day and the builder had agreed to start on the house as soon as she delivered the key to him.

She was at Paul's office even before his receptionist. He was already there, lost in cyberspace. 'Surfing the "net"?' Without meaning to she sounded facetious.

'Checking my shares.' His reply was frosty. 'My "fix" before I get stuck into the work of the day. I come in early every morning.' He got up and walked over to his desk where he collected the papers pertaining to her cottage. She already had the cheque in her hand, belatedly she realised that neither had wished the other 'good morning'.

'Bert Finley doing your renovations is he?' he asked as he handed her the keys.

'Yes, he should be there now, actually. He said he would start getting that dreadful tin lean-to down. Thank you for telling me about him, I'd better get these to him.' She opened the hand with the keys, closing her fingers tightly almost immediately, as if afraid they might take flight.

'I think you will find him a good man, very reliable, gets on with the job.' Now when she was about to walk out of his office for good he wanted to keep her there. 'Well that's it.'

'Yes, that's it!' Fern agreed, and with the comforting feel of hard metal in her hand she turned to the door. When she reached it, she paused and looked back at him. 'Thank you, thank you for—everything,'

'My job.' Then thinking how abrupt he sounded, he added, 'If you run into problems, or need any help, anything at all, get in touch.'

'Thanks,' she repeated, 'I will.' Still she hovered, torn two ways. Eager to get to her house, open up and take stock and see the work of renovating under way, at the same time finding it absurdly hard to leave.

'Well, I'd better get going.' She was turning the knob when, to her own surprise, she turned back towards him and repeated, 'Thanks again,' adding impulsively, 'You must come and see it when it's finished.'

'I'll do that,' he assured her. He would, too, he thought and hoped she caught his smile before she closed the door with a decisive click behind her.

She had, but was too busy trying to ignore its effect as she said to herself, 'I'm not running after him.' Repeating it as she got into her car, this time to the voice in her head telling her, 'Never run after a man or a bus—there is always another one coming.'

Behind her in his office Paul wondered how this oddly familiar stranger who, more often than not, gave him the brush-off, had got under his skin to the point that he wanted to run after her, apologise for his churlish manner and arrange a time to see her again.

The weeks flew in a haze of work and planning and painting. Fern was so tired at night that she simply dropped into the bed, sometimes onto it, and went out like a snuffed candle.

The paint was still tacky when she moved in, but she had given her notice on the flat and had to leave.

Walking through the rooms she was elated to see how well her alterations had worked out. The original kitchen had been turned into a charming living space with a convenient galley kitchen at one end. A small extension had given her an indoor bathroom with a shower over the old cast iron claw-footed tub. Fern was equally happy with her colour schemes, the kitchen and living area glowed in warm apricot in direct contrast to the cool greens and silvers of the bathroom. She walked through into her bedroom, now papered in a sprigged Victorian design, predominantly blue and carpeted in a deep azure that picked up the colour in the paper. She had not hesitated over the paper for, incredibly, it was the same as the original paper hanging, torn and stained, from the wall when she first saw the house. Remembering her dream, Fern knew she could not pass it by. She looked at it now, fresh and new on the walls. She knew that good patterns were often revived; even so it was an extraordinary feeling to see it there, like meeting an old friend. She wished, just for a moment, she had someone there to share her delight in the transformation.

She went to the back door, the hideous lean-to had gone, in its place was a patch of ground she planned to turn into lawn, or maybe courtyard. Dusk was falling, but in the dim light she sensed, then saw, the black and white cat watching her from the shadows. Taking her hesitation as invitation, it emerged and padded softly across the rough ground towards her, stopped a few feet away and miaowed very loudly.

'Go away—shoo!' It sat down and looked at her. Obviously, Fern decided as she turned back indoors, she had not sounded convincing. And she wasn't convinced. Deep down there was a curious feeling that the cat had as much right to be there as she had—that in some way it had always been there.

She had barely closed the door when the rain, which had threatened all day, started. The cat, wet and bedraggled, flicked through her consciousness as a loud roll of thunder coincided with the lights going out. She groped for her handbag on the kitchen stool and found the pen torch she kept inside it for such emergencies.

Fern rationalised her action by telling herself it was a subconscious need for company that made her open the door and sweep the thin beam around the wet yard until twin lights were reflected back. Instantly, it crossed the few feet between them, shot past her and into the house.

At that moment the electricity returned, and with it her common sense.

'Out!' Fern commanded, pointing to the open door. The cat simply stared back. The rain increased in ferocity and splattered through the open door. Fern felt annoyed to be outfaced and outwitted by a cat, and such a scruffy one at that. She softened, however, as she looked at the damp black fur tinged with rust, the white shirtfront spattered with mud, the whole standing up in curious peaks and tufts, the very antithesis of sleek, and realised that beneath this unkempt coat was a very thin cat. Pity clenched her heart.

'Okay, just this once, you can stay, till the rain stops.' They treated each other to a long stare. A mutual weighing up. Then Fern turned to the box of groceries she had brought from the flat to see what they could both have for supper.

Among the assorted cans she found one of baked beans, for her, and one of sardines, for the cat. He ate them ravenously. By the time they had eaten the rain had stopped. She made herself coffee and poured milk into his dish. She placed it outside the back door.

'Now,' she informed the back of his head as he lapped it up, 'you can go home, or wherever it is you came from. Letting you in was a momentary weakness. It won't happen again.' He continued to lap noisily, more like a dog than a cat. Maybe, Fern thought, it really was a long time since he had enjoyed such a luxury. She closed her mind and the door firmly. She was not into forming relationships, with people or animals. She couldn't face the pain of any more endings. She slid the bolt across and turned the heavy key in the old-fashioned lock. It was then that anticlimax hit.

Here was her great new beginning, but instead of euphoria, even satisfaction, she merely felt tired in body, flat in spirit and, yes—lonely. She had to remind herself of her determination to be self-sufficient—in every way, to stop herself calling the cat back inside.

Too tired to bathe or shower she merely brushed her teeth and fell into bed, blessing herself for having the foresight to make it up earlier in the day. That night she dreamed again, and woke screaming.

Fully awake she forced herself to remember. Particularly the people in it, and to analyse her own feelings. Why was she so afraid?

The dream had begun with the raised voice demanding that she come out from her room where she had been sewing with her maid.

She remembered carefully sticking the needle in the fabric before setting it down and rising slowly, taking deep breaths to still the wild pounding of her heart. She walked onto the landing that overlooked the stone flagged entrance hall. All her senses seemed heightened, she heard her dress rustle with a soft hiss. She held her head proudly, conscious of the thudding

37

of her heart.

Her right hand gripped the polished oak of the handrail. Below, his body foreshortened by her view of him, her husband stared up at her. Hatred and jubilation, a terrifying blend, glowed in his eyes as they met her own. She shook with loathing and fear. Two labourers from the estate stood at each end of a rough farm gate. The prone body was covered in a mud-stained cloak, an arm hung limply. On the little finger a familiar gold and onyx signet ring caught her eye. Her knuckles shone white as her grip tightened on the rail and she braced herself for the moment when the cloak was twitched back from the face.

Slowly, she tore her gaze from the dead man and looked straight at her husband. Desperately she tried to speak, to disclaim all knowledge of the man on the bier, but was unable to make a sound, paralysed by his cold eyes glittering with malice. She clawed at the handrail with her second hand, but her legs folded and grey mist swirled around her, enveloping her. The soft swish of her skirts as she fell was the last sound she heard.

Awake she tried to analyse the dream. Why the intense hatred for Nigel? She had not hated him. Far from it, although lately pity had mingled with her love. She had feared for him, occasionally feared him, but never hated him. And why such concern for the other man, the body on the pallet? A man she scarcely knew, yet who, since she came here, was constantly in her waking thoughts and now it seemed in her dreams as well.

Before she had left Melbourne her sleep had constantly been disturbed by nightmares in which Nigel featured. Or more often than not his body, and she was being forced to look at it. In this dream he had been very much alive, almost gloating as he showed her the body of—that other person. There was something else different, always before she had been in her normal, everyday clothes. She had certainly not been in sixteenth century dress nor had she been living in a country house in rural England.

The sudden and rather surprising knowledge that she knew both the time and place of her dream shocked her into a state of being very wide awake. She got out of bed and went to her handbag where she knew she would find a notepad and a pen and began to jot facts down. If she wrote everything she remembered of the dream that had so rudely awakened her then she could assess it properly next day when she was fully awake.

I am in a large country house in Herefordshire, she wrote. *My husband is the local Lord of the Manor. I am frightened of him, and I hate him. It is 1557 . . .* She looked down in astonishment at the words she had written. Why was she so sure of the place and the year? Neither had been stated specifically at any point in the dream. What was Nigel, or any of them, doing in the 16th Century?

Fern's first reaction was to consign the whole thing to the too hard basket, but there was something that made this dream different from those other terrifying nightmares. They had been a re-living of a trauma, last night's dream had been sheer fantasy, not a re-enactment of something that had already happened. If she could accept it as that it could be dismissed, forgotten. On this resolution she walked to her brand-new, and blissfully real, bathroom and stepped under the shower. She turned the taps anxiously. Joy of joys, the water was hot!

Dressed casually in jeans and sweatshirt, she flicked on the electric jug and dropped bread into the toaster. A loud wail at the door announced that her unwelcome guest was still around and, by the sound of it, expecting breakfast. A plaintive miaow just as she was pouring milk into her coffee transcended even the sound of the radio. When she opened the door, he stalked in as if he owned the place. His unwarranted confidence, so at odds with his woefully scraggy appearance, touched her. Once again she was forced to note how thin he was. Against all common sense, she offered a generous saucer of milk. He thanked her with a sound mid-way between a purr and a yowl, and began to lap noisily.

Fern sipped her coffee and looked down on

the back of his head. There was something touchingly vulnerable about that skinny neck and the over large ears. But she didn't want to feel touched. She jumped down from her stool with her empty cup and snatched up the saucer as her visitor licked the last drop.

'You can go out now,' she told him. The cat ignored her and began to wash. Fern picked him up and deposited him outside, trying to ignore the bony feel of his body. She didn't want him in her house or her life, not if he was going to make claims on her affection in any way, she told herself firmly as she washed her cup, saucer and plate and the saucer the cat had used.

She dismissed him from her thoughts, found a scrap of paper and a ballpoint pen and began to make a list of the things she needed. Cat food was not on the list. When she left the house some twenty minutes later, he was not around. She hoped he had made his way home, wherever that was.

Her first call was to the bank. When she discovered how low her reserves were after she had drawn out enough for her immediate needs, she realised the time had come to start earning again and stop spending. She had planned to write a book on interior design, but realised now she couldn't allow herself the luxury of settling down to that with no money coming in for her everyday needs. But by leaving Melbourne and coming to the country, she had also left her market. Obviously she must find new clients. Hard on this thought she found her feet began walking of their own volition towards Paul's office.

She stopped abruptly, just short of the door. What on earth was she doing, had she lost all sense of self, of her own worth, where was her much prized independence? Had Paul Denton cast a spell over her or something with his crazy greeting, his craggy good looks and the humiliating way her heart thudded when their eyes happened to meet?

No—whatever she did she would not ask him for help. With a supreme effort she continued walking—right past his door.

CHAPTER THREE

Paul looked up from his desk as Fern emerged from the bank. He watched her hesitate, glance at her watch, stand for a moment, as if deciding what to do, then with an air of determination, cross over the street. He craned forward across his desk to see whether she continued down the street or as he hoped, headed for his office. With the deal settled and done there was no reason why she should be coming to see him.

He got up and moved to the window. She was heading for his office. But, no—she had stopped almost at his door, wheeled away and was walking briskly down the street. Without stopping to think he dashed past an astonished Dot on the phone at the reception desk.

'Paul!' she called, her hand over the mouthpiece. He ignored her and, with a slight shrug, she removed her hand and assumed a diplomatic voice.

He caught up with Fern at the next corner. 'Oh—Hi!' He made a valiant attempt in spite of his breathlessness to sound casual, then blew it by adding, 'I saw you outside—I thought you were coming to the office.'

'I was,' Fern admitted, caught off guard. They were both walking again, how it had happened she wasn't sure, but they were heading back to his office.

Once more, Dot tried to claim his attention as they passed her reception desk but Paul made a 'not now—later' gesture in her direction and stood back to let Fern precede him into his office.

As she brushed past him she was so intensely aware of him that her skin actually seemed to tingle. An odd sensation, she couldn't remember anyone else affecting her in quite the same way—ever.

'Come on in, sit down.' He pulled forward a chair for her then perched on the edge of his desk.

Almost too close for comfort, Fern thought.

'Can I help you?' he asked. 'Nothing wrong

43

is there?' She looked so uptight he felt anxious.

'No nothing wrong, everything is fine.' Fern sat tensely on the edge of the chair. 'I don't know whether you can help me or not, but I couldn't think of anyone else.'

'Try me,' Paul invited.

Meeting his eyes Fern caught her breath. The mini electric shock that ran through her being was becoming familiar. She realised she was smiling broadly.

Fern pulled her mouth straight, sat taller in her seat, and tried for a level voice, as she explained. 'I need to earn some money. I plan to write a book on interior design, but of course that won't bring in anything for a long time even if I find someone willing to publish it. I guess . . .' she admitted, 'I've spent rather more than I intended on my makeover of the cottage.' She had an uncomfortable feeling that she was losing her cool, she was rambling, gabbling almost. Suddenly, what had seemed so simple didn't feel quite such a good idea. She made a move as if to get up and leave.

Paul understood. 'You need work, commissions to do other houses?'

'Yes, I just wondered if you knew of anyone needing the services of an interior designer. Perhaps someone like me—bought a house that needs renovating. Of course I could advertise, but word of mouth is always the best. So . . . or would that be unethical?' she finished when he did not answer immediately.

'No, just helpful. I recommended a man to do your renovations, and you seemed quite pleased.'

'Oh, I was, he was great and did a terrific job, got on with it too. I just wondered . . .' her voice trailed off as she opened her bag. 'I've done up some new business cards on the computer with the contact details brought up to date.' Tentatively, she passed a small bundle of cards across the desk towards Paul.

'As a matter of fact, I think I do know someone. I'll give them one of these.' He hesitated, aware of her dislike of anything that could be construed as a pass. 'I could be more convincing in my recommendation if I had seen what you have done with your own place.'

Fern stiffened. She had no desire to have him, or any man, intrude in her new independent world, but he was only talking business sense. 'I suppose you are right, you had better come and have a look.' She did her best not to sound ungracious. Paul glanced down at his watch, as keen as she was to avoid embarrassing eye contact.

'I could come now, if that suits you.'

Fern stood up. He noted, or remembered, he was not sure which, that she was almost his own height. 'Yes—of course.' Her voice was distant, businesslike, as she turned towards the door.

Paul stood up and followed her from the

office, at the same time wondering why, in spite of the cool 'back off' signals she consistently meted out to him, he wanted her company. But he felt some kind of magnetic pull, he was sure he must know her from somewhere.

*   *   *

Paul did not have to simulate any admiration for the transformation she had achieved in the old cottage. The last time he had walked through it had seemed to him almost impossible that such a dank depressing place could ever be made liveable. He could barely credit that this bright cottage, sparkling with old world charm blended with modern comfort and convenience, was the same place. Even he, who saw a surfeit of 'desirable residences' in his work, was impressed as he followed her from room to room.

'Well, what do you think?' Fern broke the silence, which was becoming uncomfortable. They were standing in her bedroom and he was staring at the pretty blue and white sprigged paper, frowning slightly. 'Don't you like this paper?'

'Yes—yes . . .' He half turned towards her, still frowning and shaking his head as if puzzled. 'It is beautiful. I am just trying to remember where I have seen it before.'

She laughed, 'It was the original paper, so

46

you have seen it, but it didn't look quite like this.'

Paul turned to her. 'It is as familiar to me as . . .' He had been about to say, 'you were when I first saw you', but finished the sentence lamely with, 'my own face in the mirror.'

'I know they often re-issue old designs but I didn't expect to come across it straight away,' Fern told him.

'It's a pretty paper,' he murmured, 'I am quite sure I have seen it somewhere before.' He frowned slightly, trying to remember.

Paul dismissed the paper from his mind, the memory would surface one day he was sure. 'Do you want to sell?' his smile was teasing.

'No way!' Fern was emphatic. But she smiled back, acknowledging the compliment. 'You are impressed then?'

'Absolutely. To be honest I thought you were mad buying this place, in fact I felt rather guilty selling it to you. But I take my hat off to you, you've done a wonderful job.' They had moved back into the pleasant living space with its bright, practical galley kitchen and he thought of the disaster area it had been. 'I hope you took some "before" and "after" shots?'

'Lashings of them—before, after and some "work in progress" ones too,' Fern assured him. 'I have been in this business long enough to know that to really convince people what you can do you have to show them what you

47

started with as well as the finished product.'

Paul had only been half listening to her, he had been running over in his mind various ways of asking her to have lunch with him. But enough of what she was saying had filtered through to remind him that he had promised to find more clients for her. He punched a number into his mobile phone. Fern had moved slightly away but she guessed from the tone of his voice that he was leaving a message. 'I have asked them to call me back, if you could meet me for lunch, I will probably have spoken to them by then.' To his surprise the invitation had slipped out naturally.

Fern found herself mumbling something vague and indecisive.

'Good . . .' Paul glanced at his watch, 'I'll meet you in—say an hour—at the pub?' He stuffed his phone back in his pocket and added regretfully, 'I suppose I had better get back to the office . . . I'll see you later.'

'Yes . . .' Fern agreed, she was thinking about Dot who had obviously wanted Paul's attention, then realised that her agreement had been taken as acceptance of his invitation to join him for lunch. She wasn't sure she wanted that, but lunch with a person hardly constituted an emotional tie, and it was good to have praise for her work, it would be churlish, even foolish to refuse if he could give her introductions to other clients, so she let it stand.

Good grief, she thought as she riffled through her limited wardrobe, if only she had brought some decent clothes. It might be the country, but she would still like to look her stylish best. Then she shrugged, what does it matter, it is only business after all, she tried to convince herself, if only he would stop looking at her with those smiling eyes.

*   *   *

'We must drink to your success,' Paul insisted as they settled at a corner table.

'Just one glass,' she acquiesced, when he asked her whether she would prefer white or red wine, 'or I shall spend the afternoon asleep.'

'Just one glass,' he agreed, 'I have clients to see.' They smiled at each other across the table like old friends sharing a well-worn joke.

'I can't shake off the feeling that we've met somewhere.' Paul's words swept away the pleasant feeling of relaxed camaraderie.

'I don't think so,' Fern retorted, her voice chilling by degrees. Surely he wasn't about to harp on that corny line again. She was tempted to suggest he could do better. She knew they had never met. She would have remembered.

She looked down, refusing to meet his searching eyes, then suddenly, her breath caught in a sharp gasp as she noticed the signet ring on his little finger.

49

Gold and onyx.

Like the body on the makeshift stretcher in her dream. But it was only a dream, wasn't it?

'I am quite sure we have never met,' she snapped. She had no intention of telling him about her bizarre dream and letting him think that she was responding to his pass, or worse, making one herself. The comfortable atmosphere had dissolved and they finished their meal making polite and stilted conversation. They parted with mutual relief.

Only as he walked back to his office did Paul remember that he had not told her he had already given her number to a possible client. It was a genuine lapse of memory—all the same . . . He toyed with the idea of calling her but a hectic schedule of appointments kept him busy. He remembered his omission when Dot ushered Fiona Cameron into his office.

*   *   *

Fern set up her laptop on her dining table. She was determined to think of anything but the disturbingly attractive man she had just left and his appearance in both her everyday life and her dreams. A lowering sky threatening rain kept her indoors. Needing a counter irritant to the disturbing effect Paul seemed to be having on her mind, she decided to work on her ideas for the book on interior design. She was totally absorbed in sorting out photos and getting rough ideas down when the phone rang.

'Hello,' she rapped, annoyed at the interruption. 'Oh, Paul. Hi.' She took a deep breath and waited for him to speak.

'I have Fiona Cameron with me, I left a message on her mobile. She has just bought an old farm property and needs advice on how best to do it up. She has one of your cards but would like to talk to you, can you spare a moment?'

'Of course,' Fern assured him, repressing her initial resentment at this interruption of her burst of creativity.

'It's Fiona Cameron,' Paul repeated, his voice implying the name would be familiar to her. 'I'll put her on.'

After a slight pause, a woman's voice, slightly husky and unusually deep, came on the line. Fern got the impression that she was fairly young. She agreed to look at the old homestead the following morning. She was elated at the prospect of the work but the interruption had broken her creative mood. She shut down her computer and pushed her books and papers to one side. A cup of tea seemed like a good idea and she got up from the table to brew herself one. The storm that had threatened earlier had dissolved and a pale sun was now breaking through the clouds. She opened the door taking deep breaths of the cool fresh air.

As she stepped outside, the cat came out from the thick, unkempt bit of garden with its overgrown shrubs near the door. It greeted her with a harsh and singularly un-musical miaow.

'So—you're back?' Fern wondered if it were back or if it had never been away. Its answering yowl could have meant either. It had the most strident voice she had ever heard, but it certainly got attention. She almost regretted her failure to include cat food in her shopping list. 'Why don't you go back home?' she demanded. 'You can't stay here. I don't want you or need you. I don't want or need anyone any more, ever again. I am self-sufficient, like you.' She studied the half-starved, scraggy creature in front of her and amended it to, 'Like cats are supposed to be,' as it sat down and stared at her. Just as if she, not it, were the interloper. For a crazy moment she felt it was right, or at least that it belonged here as much as she did.

It took advantage of her lack of attention to slip into the kitchen with her. Fern poured out a generous saucer of milk, it seemed the thing to do when she had a drink herself.

Leaving the back door open, she carried her tea outside and parked herself on an upturned milk crate left behind by the previous owner. It would be a good idea, she thought, to treat herself to some garden furniture. The cat followed her out, a pearly droplet of milk suspended from its chin. It sat down in a patch of watery sunlight to wash. Fern felt unexpected empathy; like her, it was endeavouring to pick itself up off the scrap heap of life. Perhaps she would buy cat food next time she was at the shops.

Fern drained her tea, put her cup down on the milk crate, and strolled round her new domain. The pruned roses were now in bud and the pansies she had planted were already turning smiling faces towards the sun. The garden, like the house, was beginning to have a cared for look. Idly, she pulled a weed out here, broke off a dead flowering head there and soaked up the serenity of this little patch of earth that was now hers and hers alone.

All signs of bad weather had now fled and the sun, even though it was late afternoon or early evening, according to your personal reckoning, had gained in both strength and warmth. Fern went to her little garden shed and collected shears and garden gloves and began to attack the overgrown wilderness at her back door. The cat watched her.

Inexorably, her thoughts turned to Paul. He had referred a new client to her after all. But Fern wondered why her mind seemed to find her way back to him each time. Her relationship with Paul was strictly business after all. *But what about the ring?* her recalcitrant mind wondered. Why was the dead man in her dream wearing the exact same ring as Paul? Had she noticed it subconsciously and featured it in her dream? She didn't think so, she certainly hadn't noticed it before. What then?

A shiver ran up Fern's spine and she noticed that the light had begun to wane. She was both tired and hungry, but also satisfied with her efforts. Cooking a meal for one presented altogether too great an effort. She looked at the cat, it looked back and gave one of its deep throated yowls as if it were pointing out to her that there were two people who needed a meal.

Alone she might have made do with toast and Vegemite, faced with a hungry cat, fish and chips from the shop in the main street was a better option.

She gave the cat his portion of fish and took her own along with a can of light ale into the small lounge where she relaxed in front of the TV to watch the news.

It was, as usual, depressing. As she was only using it as background noise, she flicked it off and put a CD on instead. Briefly, inner peace flowed through her senses as Chopin's Raindrop Prelude flowed around her. Though she had not actually been working, as in career, the work she had put in on the old cottage to transform it from an unkempt shell into the attractive home it was today had been a challenge. As with every job she had ever done, she had learned something from it.

This line of thought inevitably made her

think of the next day and she felt a frisson of pleasurable excitement at the promise of new work. It was a long time since she had felt this way.

She got out her folder of 'before and after' photographs. Looking at the wreck she had started with, it hardly seemed possible that this was the same house. She would take this particular folder along with her tomorrow when she went out to see Fiona Cameron's farmhouse.

Steeling her heart, she put the cat out before she went to bed. His presence had contributed to her relaxed mood, which helped her fall asleep quickly, looking forward to the coming day. Yet she woke in a cold sweat of terror from the now familiar dream.

Once again she'd been wearing old-fashioned clothes, a maroon dress, a colour that she avoided, in fact actively disliked. As before she stared down on the rough bier. She knew who lay there long before she saw the onyx ring. She shook her head in an attempt to rid herself of the feeling of shock, horror and nameless terror that she carried with her from the dream as she opened her eyes to a glorious early summer morning in Australia in the twenty-first century. Slowly, she subsided on her pillows and concentrated on the pretty sprigged pattern of her bedroom wallpaper instead of the nightmare. As the dream slid away another, half waking half sleeping, fantasy took over.

She felt that she was standing at the front door of her cottage. It was early morning, before sunrise, and the lamplight inside shone through the flannel flower glass over the door, casting a slight rosy hue on the soldier wearing the uniform of a private in the First World War. He held her in a last tight embrace; she felt the coarseness of the cloth against her bare arms. The ache in her heart was unbearable as he released her. Only when the gate clicked shut behind him did she turn back to the house. She knew this was 'Goodbye'. An ugly white and black cat wove round her feet as she turned back into the house.

Drowsily, Fern wondered if she had picked up the vibrations of an earlier occupant of the cottage? She snatched at this explanation and tried to dismiss the memory of seeing that damned onyx ring again and the disturbing conviction that the soldier was Paul. And the cat. There was no mistaking it. Fern shook her head, clearing away the cobwebs clinging to her mind from out of time.

Enough of dreams and fantasies, she would soon not be able to distinguish them from reality and she had promised Fiona Cameron to be there at eleven o'clock. She jumped out of bed, snatched up bra, pants and bathrobe and headed for the shower.

Half an hour later, with her newly shampooed hair in damp tendrils around her face and dressed only in undies and bathrobe, she was in her narrow galley kitchen, making toast and coffee, as she listened to the radio dispensing its regular dose of gloom and doom disguised as the nine a.m. news. She wondered if the cat was hoping for brekky and went to the door to see if it was there.

At the precise moment that Fern opened the door, Paul raised his hand to knock on it. Confronted by a male fist apparently about to punch her in the face, she stepped smartly back with a yelp of shock and surprise.

'Sorry, I didn't mean to startle you.' His voice sounded contrite but there was a gleam of amusement in his eyes.

'Well you did!' Fern snapped.

The cat, ever an opportunist, shot indoors. Fern registered this with a tiny part of her mind. She was grappling with Paul's totally unexpected appearance in the flesh so soon after her night-time fantasies.

'Sorry,' he repeated, looking anything but. Fern felt herself colouring as her loosely tied robe gaped open, revealing how little she had on underneath. Snatching it closed she pulled the tie belt so vigorously it made her gasp.

'What do you want?' The churlish note in her own voice, and her innate good manners, prompted her to add, not too graciously, 'Come in.'

She half hoped he would refuse, but he followed her to the kitchen where the cat was mewing loud and long.

'I see you have adopted Bill Smith's cat,' he said, stooping to scratch the dome of its head. 'I'm glad; it took off to fend for itself when the old boy was carted off to the Home. I think he worried, he was fond of it.'

'*It* has adopted *me*.' Fern poured milk into a saucer and held it out to Paul.

'For me?' His eyes gleamed with barely concealed amusement.

'For the cat,' she snapped. She had no intention of bending down and giving him an even better view of her cleavage.

His lips twitched as he took it from her and placed it carefully in front of the cat.

Straightening up Paul was assailed by the tempting smells of coffee and toast.

His loud sniff was as blatant as the cat's yowl.

'I suppose you would like coffee?' Fern pushed the plunger down as she spoke.

'Please!'

'And toast?' she hovered over the toaster with two more slices.

'Yes, please,' he ignored or simply did not hear the inflection in her voice.

Fern dropped two slices into the slots and pressed down the lever.

'I find it really hard to believe what you've done with this place,' he told her as he took the proffered coffee from her. 'You have really made the most of your space with this galley kitchen opening off the living area.'

'Flattery will get you everywhere!' Fern quipped, regretting the words even as she spoke. Now he would surely think that she was making a pass. She wondered, as she put the toast on the table, what had brought him here so early in the day.

'I came to see if you would like a lift to the Camerons',' he explained as he helped himself to honey. She sat down opposite him thinking, briefly, that it seemed quite natural to be breakfasting together, and at the same time wondering why he hadn't just used the phone.

'Thanks, but Fiona gave me directions. It was kind of you to give me the introduction, you don't have to take me there as well.'

'I was going anyway. But if . . .' he shrugged as if dismissing the subject.

Fern recognised that she was being unnecessarily ungracious, after all, a personal introduction could do no harm. 'Oh, well—in that case—if you really wouldn't be making a special journey . . .' she trailed off, hoping he would not accept her refusal.

Glancing at his watch, he pushed his chair back. 'I must go, I have an appointment.'

The feeling of domestic bliss instantly disappearing, Fern felt strangely miffed at his hurried departure.

'I think I dreamed about you last night.' Fern was aghast, what had possessed her to say that?

She wondered if he had heard when he turned at the door and said, 'Thanks for the breakfast. I'll be here about twenty minutes to eleven.' But in the doorway he turned back. 'Was it a nice dream?' he asked.

'No,' she snapped, his faintly mocking smile catching her on the raw, but he was gone before she got the word out.

Fern tingled with anticipation laced with anxiety as she prepared herself to meet the Camerons. It was months since she had worked for a client. Doing up her own cottage had been therapy. Preoccupation with her alterations combined with the quiet tempo of this little country town, so similar to that of the rural Tasmanian community where she had grown up, had worked wonders. She hoped taking on paid work would not shatter her new, and rather fragile, confidence.

She dressed first in a smart navy suit and white shirt, businesslike and efficient. Then decided it was too formal and citified to look over an old farmhouse and replaced it with a more casual, but still elegant, pants suit. She was still re-doing her hair when she heard Paul draw up at the gate. Ramming her folder into her briefcase, she ran out to meet him.

'They are nice folk, the Camerons, I've known them for a while,' Paul told her, surprised to see her so flustered.

'Oh, they're not just clients then?'

'Yes, and no. They are clients, but not

"just". Alex and I met briefly at primary school, his family were living in New Zealand then, and our paths have had a tendency to cross, equally briefly, ever since,' he told her.

'Primary school—that is way back.' She smiled to soften what she suddenly felt might sound like a suggestion that he was over the hill. For a second their eyes met and once more she felt that flick of recognition. Both looked away quickly, Fern because she didn't want recognition or any other emotion to cloud the easy 'take it or leave it' relationship they had, Paul because having received what he felt to be the ice maiden treatment from her before had no wish to repeat the experience. Nor had he any desire to be emotionally involved with her or anyone else.

His mind told him that in a 'no nonsense' way, but his body told him something quite different. Her physical nearness made all his nerve ends tingle. He concentrated on driving and remained silent for the rest of the journey.

Fern admired the scenery, and wondered whether to tell him of her dream. She decided not to, unless he asked. He didn't, she wasn't sure whether she was glad or sorry, but, *'least said, soonest mended,'* she decided.

Fern was surprised when she stepped out of the car in front of a rambling old house giving the odd impression that a giant hand had plonked it down. 'I thought it was a farm property,' she said to Paul, 'how come there are no yards or sheds?'

'They bought a couple of paddocks then purchased the house, you know one of those removal ones, and had it set up here,' Paul explained.

'Ahh . . .' Fern sighed, that explained its dumped down look. She was about to say that to Paul, but he was looking beyond her and waving to a man who had just appeared from the back of the house. Fern almost repeated her '*Aah*' as he drew closer. He was the most strikingly handsome man she had ever seen off the stage or the celluloid screen. What she would call 'drop dead gorgeous', what Gran would have described as a Greek God. Tall and blonde with a slight wave in his hair, perfectly sculptured features, true blue eyes and a skin that was tanned evenly to a light bronze. Unusual in someone so fair. Obviously this was not Fiona. As her focus moved from the man to his surroundings, the front door opened and a fashionably clipped small white poodle erupted and hurtled towards them. A young woman ran after it, her mane of thick golden hair had just enough red in it to give the impression of an iridescent halo as she moved into the brilliant mid-day sun.

'Paul—how marvellous—you've brought Fern.'

'I've brought Fern . . .' he agreed and seemed to think this was sufficient introduction as he caught Fiona in a great bear hug. 'You look terrific—as always,' he told her as he released her.

Only then did they become aware of the poodle yipping and dancing excitedly around the group. Paul bent to pet the animal, not noticing that Fern was standing stiffly, her lips unsmiling.

But Fiona, with a warm smile and outstretched hand, quickly introduced herself, 'I'm Fiona, and this is Alex—but I expect you already guessed that. And this is Beau, don't let him bother you, I promise he won't bite.' She laughed at the sheer absurdity of such a notion.

'No, no—I am sure he won't, it's just that . . .' but how explain? Fern forced her stiff lips to smile and attempted to regain her savoir-faire.

'You don't like dogs?' Paul, who loved them, sounded amazed.

Before she could answer, Fiona picked up the hyperactive little poodle. 'Fern Barclay!' she breathed in that incredible husky voice, remembered from the phone. 'Come to the rescue, how wonderful that Paul knew you and could persuade you to help. Come inside—and tell us what we must do to make this place fit to live in.'

As they went through the door, Fiona took her arm and said in a confidential voice, 'He tells me you are a genius, Fern, that you have achieved miracles with the house he sold you.'

Fern was not sure how to answer this. If she simply said, 'Yes,' she would be claiming to be a miracle worker on one hand and something of a pushover to let anyone sell her such a rotten house on the other. So she simply smiled and allowed herself to be propelled inside what she could see immediately was not anything like the wreck her cottage had been when she had first seen it and against all sense and reason fallen in love with it.

As they entered the wide entrance hall leading to the kitchen they were met by the wonderful smell of brewing coffee. The poodle, which Fiona had released from her arms, kept close to its mistress's heels. Fern saw that a shining copper coloured percolator was perking merrily on the stove, hence the wonderful aroma. Plungers, she thought, as Fiona placed the percolator on a trolley already laid with cups, saucers, sugar, cream, and shortbread biscuits, were convenient but they didn't emit such a fantastic waft of coffee fragrance.

'I thought we would prime up with caffeine before we got down to business.' Fiona threw her a wide smile as she trundled the trolley through to the lounge room. Fern, responding to her warmth, returned the smile and followed.

She let her eyes rove around the room. Everything appeared to be structurally sound and there were no obvious disasters, such as the peeling wallpaper that she had found in her cottage. In fact, for many people there would have been nothing wrong with this house. She sipped her coffee, accepted shortbread and waited for Fiona to start the ball rolling.

She seemed in no hurry, but chatted to Paul, leaving Fern to answer Alex's questions.

'About three months,' she told him when he asked how long she had been living in the district, 'but I haven't been in my cottage that long. I rented a flatlet till I could move in. There were a lot of structural changes, things like a new bathroom and kitchen.'

'I see you have brought a folder with you.' It was lying on the sofa at Fern's side. 'Have you any photos of your house?'

'Before and after ones.' Fern smiled, as she put down her empty coffee cup. 'Would you like to see them?'

'Please.' Alex quickly crossed the room to join her on the sofa. Fern subconsciously moved a couple of inches away from him as she reached for the folder and flipped it open.

'I have them arranged in rooms. Before and after together,' she told him as she passed it to him.

'I like these,' he exclaimed after a few minutes silent inspection. 'They live up to your reputation. Fiona, stop gossiping and take a look.'

Fiona studied them carefully. In the silence,

Fern glanced across at Paul. He was leaning back in his chair with the sort of expression on his face that proud parents wore when their offspring were doing something well. She found it very irritating; she was not a child but a professional with an established reputation. She forgot that she had asked Paul for his help in finding work and her reputation probably didn't extend so far from the metropolis as this rural backwater.

'These sure look good,' Fiona conceded. 'Could I see the real thing?' she asked as she handed the folder back.

'But of course—any time.' Fern would have shown her photos of some of the other places she had done. But Fiona jumped to her feet.

'Come along and I'll give you the grand tour and explain the sort of effect I want.'

Fern followed the younger woman, looking around with interest. It was a fairly typical farmhouse, the paintwork, carpets etc., were all in good order, although in Fern's eyes, sadly lacking in taste. She gave a little shudder as she looked down at the wall-to-wall carpet patterned in an over colourful floral design. Except for some overblown roses it was anyone's guess just what the flowers were.

Fiona noticed her reaction and smiled. 'Appalling isn't it? Now, bearing in mind that this is a holiday house not a permanent home, I want it done in a relaxed but tasteful and restful manner. We both have a pretty stressful lifestyle and we want this to be our haven, our space to revive in, our resuscitation pad, and our holiday home. Our bolt hole when we are in danger of getting stressed out.'

'I get your drift,' Fern assured her with a smile. 'You won't be living here permanently?'

'Definitely not! We may bring visitors sometimes, we will need a functional kitchen, an extra bathroom, that sort of thing.'

Fern looked around thoughtfully then scribbled ideas on her notepad. Her professional interest and enthusiasm stirred as she realised this presented more of a challenge than suggesting colour schemes. Just what she needed now her own home was completed. Working on the transformation of this house would leave little time to think about the recent past—or anything else. It would be good, too, to know someone else in the area. She was in danger of relying too much on Paul. She had felt an immediate rapport with Fiona and felt they might become good friends.

And Alex . . . so good looking . . . yet, somehow Fern felt a little uncomfortable in his presence. There seemed to be no reason for this, he had been urbane and charming, but somehow . . . Fern mentally shook her head and glanced at her new acquaintance, speaking animatedly with Paul. There was an obvious rapport between the two and Fern could not help but wonder about their relationship.

She looked again at Alex and Fiona and

thought what a handsome couple they were. This job was going to be just the tonic she needed.

But why did the prospect of seeing less of Paul depress her?

CHAPTER FOUR

'Sorry Fern, but time is moving on and I have an appointment in . . .' Paul consulted his watch, 'twenty one minutes time.'

'Of course.' Fern closed her notebook and turned to Fiona. 'I'll work out some ideas for you straight away.'

'Terrific. We can look at them tomorrow when we come to see your place.'

'Sure, come for morning coffee.' Fern wondered if this, perhaps, was rather rash, maybe it would have been better to suggest afternoon tea, she would have to put her skates on to get some ideas and possible colour schemes worked out overnight.

'What great people, thanks for the introduction,' Fern said to Paul as they drove away.

'They are—and so is Beau.' Fern tried to ignore this but Paul persisted. 'The dog, Beau is the dog's name.'

'I know.' Fern turned to look at the scenery. 'I had no idea this was a grape growing area.'

'Surely such a small and blatantly harmless little dog couldn't strike terror in anyone's heart?' Paul was not to be deflected.

Fern continued to look out of the window. Let him think she was afraid if he wanted to. She tightened her lips and did not answer.

'Beau is utterly harmless, I should have thought you could see that.'

Fern thought he was like a dog himself, give him something to chew on and he would never let go.

'I can assure you I was not in the least afraid of him.' She hoped that the tone of her voice would make it clear she did not wish to pursue the subject.

No such luck. 'Then why—?' he began, but Fern had had enough.

'What business is it of yours, anyway?' she snapped, 'Fiona is my client, not her dog.'

'Agreed, but there is something in the adage, *Love me—love my dog.*'

'You think I may have . . . offended Fiona?'

Paul shrugged, refusing to be drawn any further into what looked as if it could develop into a stupid quarrel. He kept silent but he could not forget how the colour had drained from her face when Beau erupted onto the scene.

Fern eventually broke the silence with a change of subject. 'What does Alex Cameron do?' she asked, it was obvious that whatever it was he was not short of cash.

'Alex? Oh, he is a psychologist. Does all right; but Fiona earns most of the money as you would expect.'

'Oh, would I?' Fern sounded puzzled, this was the first time she had met either of them.

Paul looked amused. 'Didn't you recognise Fiona?'

'Should I? Is she famous or something?'

'She is Fiona Cameron.'

'Yes, I did get her name. Should it mean anything to me?'

'The Country & Western star,' Paul told her patiently.

'Ohhh!' Fern never listened to Country, or indeed any Pop music from choice.

'Are you telling me you have never heard of her?' Paul sounded disbelieving.

'Well, yes,' Fern admitted. 'If I have heard of her it didn't register. I don't usually listen to that kind of music.' How stuffy and pompous she sounded. 'I only listen to classical music,' she explained knowing she was doing little to improve matters.

'I guess you had better remedy that before you see her tomorrow,' Paul told her with a wry grin. 'Total ignorance of her reputation would not seem tactful, especially as she has heard of you and your reputation as an interior designer.'

'How am I going to know something about her overnight?' she asked. 'How did she learn about me?'

'Oh, you did a house for somebody she knows, she was impressed. There are a couple of her recordings in that CD wallet, take them home with you tonight and listen to them.'

'Thanks, I will.' Fern was genuinely grateful.

The covers were adorned with a photograph of Fiona wearing the sort of exotic and impractical outfit that no genuine bush girl would dream of wearing but which, nevertheless, made her look a million dollars.

'You might even enjoy listening to them—I do,' Paul remarked dryly. He drove in silence for a few minutes then, 'Do you mind if I drop you in the middle of the town?' he asked. 'I am cutting it pretty fine for my appointment.' He reached into the glove compartment and passed her a flyer. 'Take this with you, it might be a help, it's a floor plan of the Camerons' house,' he explained.

'Oh, it will!' Fern assured him as she climbed out of the car. 'Thanks for the lift—and for the CDs. I'll drop them back in your office when I have listened to them.'

Eager to get back to her cottage and start work on her ideas for the Cameron house, Fern shopped as quickly as she could, including cat food this time. She made herself a toasted cheese sandwich and a large mug of coffee and settled down at the kitchen table with her notes, the floor plan, and her lap-top to eat, work and listen at the same time.

What a great project, she thought, and such

lovely new clients. They seemed to have it all, good looks, good jobs, and, soon, a nice home. She wondered how Paul had come to know them. He had seemed very close to Fiona. Or maybe it was just Fern's imagination. What did she care anyway, he was so exasperating. Why did he have to push the point about Fiona's dog? It really was none of his business whether she liked dogs or not. If only it were that simple . . .

*   *   *

Paul's clients were not on time for their appointment. He sat at his desk waiting for them, not exactly twiddling his thumbs but thinking about Fern Barclay. He went back to that first meeting and felt hot with embarrassment when he recalled the extraordinary way he had behaved. Looking back he could not imagine what had got into him.

He realised now that he had never met her before: their lives had not crossed in any part of the world, and yet . . . She was an enigma to him. He wondered why, if she was as successful as Fiona seemed to think, she would choose to leave the city and bury herself in a little place like Elmore where work would, at best, be sparse, at worst non-existent. He had thought her the epitome of cool sophistication yet the sight of Fiona's dog seemed to throw her completely.

Fern Barclay, and her mixed up emotion, he decided, were taking up altogether too much of his thinking time. With a mental shake he concentrated on gathering the relevant information on the houses his new clients wanted to see. He could hear them in the outer office now.

*   *   *

Fern studied the floor plan of the Cameron house. Her first priority was to work out where to put the extra bathroom they required. As she worked she was distracted by Fiona's rich voice with its husky overtones, it seemed to fill the small room, and even though Fern claimed that this was 'not her kind of music' she found she was not only listening, but enjoying.

By the end of the afternoon she had re-designed the floor plan. By cutting off part of an unnecessarily large central hallway and passage she had worked another bathroom in and re-designed the kitchen so that it had a large dining area and yet retained a country kitchen look. There was little she could do at this stage but wait for Fiona to see and approve, or not.

Fiona did approve when she arrived next morning and she positively raved about Fern's 'darling little home'. Alex was much more restrained. Fern, studying him over her coffee

73

cup, was once more struck by his classic good looks. Had she not known otherwise she would have thought that he, not Fiona, was the one in showbusiness. She was surprised that he and Fiona should have chosen one another for they seemed so utterly dissimilar, Alex the self-contained professional, while Fiona was the outgoing extrovert artist. Maybe that, after all, was the secret of their appeal for each other.

Fern felt relaxed with Alex, she could enjoy his stunning looks without the faintest tremor. In direct contrast whenever she was with Paul she became stiff and formal in her efforts to hide from him the devastating effect he had on her. Ever since that astonishing moment when they first met, she felt as if she had just run a mile, her heart pumping, her palms sweaty and her breath ragged, as soon as she was in his orbit. Feeling herself respond to Fiona's outgoing personality she wondered about Paul's friendship with them and hoped that it was because of his long time acquaintance with Alex.

'I love what you have done with this place,' Fiona enthused. 'I can see that you have ideas, and that is why I want you to do our house. You will take it on, won't you, Fern?'

'I—I guess so,' Fern stammered. After doing nothing for so long it was a bit overwhelming to find she had won such a commission with such ease. She knew full well the importance of making a success of this, for if Fiona was pleased, she would surely tell her friends who the designer was and it might well bring more work her way.

'I'd like to know for sure, I have to go back to Melbourne tomorrow because I am off on tour for six weeks. Alex will probably come up at weekends, so any problems that crop up, you can discuss with him. Apart from that, the place will be yours, no-one to get in your hair. Could it be done in six weeks? Paul seems to know tradesmen who can do the work if you can see they carry out your ideas.'

'Yes. I should be able to.' Fern hoped she wasn't being too optimistic. 'I will do my best anyway.' Fiona's enthusiasm and eagerness swept her along and gave her the confidence to take on the task.

'Terrific!' Fiona enthused. 'Now I can relax and really enjoy my tour.'

'Are you going overseas?' Fern wanted to know.

'Not this time. Just around Australia. However,' she continued, 'there's a chance of Nashville at the end of this year or beginning of next.'

'Oh,' Fern looked blank and Fiona threw back her head and laughed.

'I can see by your expression you have no idea what that means.'

'No, I haven't,' Fern admitted.

'Nashville is the capital of the world of country music.' Alex, who had so far taken little or no part in the discussion, explained. 'It is the Mecca for people like Fiona, they must get there at least once in a lifetime.'

I—I see,' Fern murmured. This was a whole new scene for her. She would like to tell Fiona that she enjoyed her singing without admitting that she had never heard of her until Paul had lent her his CDs. But Fiona jumped to her feet exclaiming, 'I must go, why don't you have dinner with us tonight? Bring along your laptop and we will go through some colour schemes with that software you were telling me about.' Fern recognised this as part of the job, not a social invitation, and accepted.

'You have had a royal summons too, have you?' she couldn't resist saying when Paul rang a little later offering her a lift.

'If you mean I have been invited to dinner, yes.' Good manners and the fact that Fiona had suggested it when she called him made him phone. He ignored the fact that he had jumped at the chance to contact her in spite of the rather chilly reception most of his overtures received. Bearing this in mind his voice was deliberately casual. 'If you would like a lift, I'll be there just after seven.'

'Thanks, I'll be ready.' Matching coolness with polite frostiness. Pointless to cut off her nose to spite her face. She replaced the receiver firmly and tried with equal determination to dismiss Paul from her mind as she returned to her notes and her computer.

It took all her willpower.

To her annoyance she was finding it as hard to keep Paul out of her thoughts as it had been to keep the cat out of her life. Several tins of cat food now stood on her pantry shelf, silent testimony to her weakness. The cat probably considered she was the interloper, after all, he had lived here long before her. She could not think of a similar excuse for allowing Paul to dominate her thoughts.

As they had been invited to dinner, Fern had abandoned her jeans and workmanlike shirts for a skirt, albeit still navy denim, and an emerald green shirt which was an old favourite. She always felt good in it, knowing that the brilliant colour really did something for her. She rummaged in her jewel case for a pair of pearl drop earrings she usually wore with it in the evenings, glanced for a moment at the diamond ring, her engagement ring, sitting in the ring slot, then closed the lid firmly.

She slipped her notes inside her briefcase, zipped up the bag containing her laptop and was ready and waiting when Paul drew up at the gate.

'You're a punctual soul,' he approved.

'So are you,' she returned the compliment. 'I was brought up on a dairy farm, cows are sticklers for routine and the milk tanker waits for no man.'

'So—you are a country girl, that would

explain what you are doing in a place like Elmore.'

Fern fielded his remark with a question of her own, 'What brings you here?' she asked.

In the ensuing silence, Fern glanced sideways at him. She was sure he had heard her, but his face was expressionless, his eyes on the road ahead.

'Have you brought along some good ideas?' he asked, just when Fern felt she must break the silence herself. Obviously she had encroached on a no-go zone. She wondered what raw nerve she could have rubbed? Why would he be reluctant to answer? What was the big secret? Unable to ask, she simply allowed the subject to change.

'I think so, I hope Fiona will like them.'

As Paul braked outside the front door of the old farm homestead, Fern looked at it with different eyes, professional eyes. Although the interior was her business she wanted to absorb the feel and look of the whole place so that the two blended and became one harmonious whole. In the softer evening light, it did not appear so starkly 'put down' in the landscape. She could almost imagine the clump of old trees leaning to enfold it in a protective embrace.

Her thoughts were reflected in her smile as she turned to Paul. It transformed her, he thought, and smiled back. For a second their eyes held and something rare and magical flashed between them. *No relationships*, Fern reminded herself and quickly turned away. Gathering up her things, she stepped out of the car to be greeted by the Camerons, Beau bouncing at Fiona's side. Obviously recalling Fern's reactions the first time she had seen the little dog, she swiftly scooped him up in her arms.

'Come on in and have a drink, I'm dying to see your ideas.' Fiona led the way to the open front door. 'After seeing your own place I am agog to see your ideas for this.'

'I have some suggestions for you, I hope you will like some of them at least,' Fern answered judiciously. In the lounge room Fiona swept a clear space on the long low coffee table to make space for Fern to put down her folder and her laptop. 'Oh, a fruit juice, please,' she told Alex when he asked her what she would like to drink. She never thought it a good idea to mix alcohol and business, besides she was really thirsty.

'I have gin, vodka, sherry, wine cooler—just about anything.' She wondered if he had heard her as he waved a hand vaguely in the direction of the laden drinks trolley, until he added, 'even fruit juices if you insist.' Casting a quick glance over the bottles to see if she could locate a pineapple juice, Fern saw Paul looking at her with a puzzled frown which disappeared as their eyes met. She returned his glance with a cool half smile.

'Fern isn't a great drinker—never was.' As he spoke Paul realised he was again talking as if he had known Fern intimately from way back. She felt the warm colour creeping up her neck and throat as she met Alex's quizzical glance.

'I've mostly worked on my ideas for the kitchen,' Fern rushed in breathlessly to cover her embarrassment. 'I always feel it is so important to any house.'

'And this one is pretty awful at the moment, isn't it?' Fiona, who didn't appear to have noticed Paul's odd remark, cut in. 'I really hate it, but I couldn't see quite what to do with it.' She leaned forward eagerly to look at Fern's drawings. 'You've turned the whole room around!' she exclaimed.

'Only on paper,' Fern reassured her. 'Just a suggestion, I can easily think again if you don't like it.'

'I think it looks terrific,' Fiona assured her. 'I just wonder why on earth I hadn't thought of it myself, especially when I am at that awful sink with nothing but a wall to look at. Not . . .' she added as she jumped to her feet, 'that I spend much time at the sink if I can possibly help it. Come into the kitchen and show me exactly what you plan to do.'

'First and foremost I would move the sink. Take it out of that corner, which surely must give the person washing up claustrophobia, and move it round to the left under the

80

window. It's such a lovely view; you might as well enjoy it. The electric stove I would have here, that way you wouldn't have to walk across the kitchen with pans and dishes of hot food. Put the fridge where the sink is, then everything would be handy and together.'

Fern looked around frowning. A malevolent hand might have designed the huge kitchen for major inconvenience.

'Where do you plan to eat?' she asked Fiona who looked back blankly.

'Eat—when—what do you mean?'

'Sorry!' Fern laughed. 'What I really meant was do you plan a dining room or will you use the kitchen?'

'Well, we have been taking a trolley into the lounge and eating off our laps. I sort of thought of this as a temporary thing until we had a proper dining room.'

'Why not have a breakfast bar work bench across there, cutting off that part and making it into a compact galley type kitchen, along the same lines as mine, and furnish this area as a dining room? Look, I'll show you what I mean.' With a few swift strokes she sketched a rough plan. 'Different furniture of course.' She gestured towards the Formica and chrome table and chairs. 'There is some wonderful fruitwood furniture around these days, it looks terrific in country kitchens.'

'I went for functionality,' Fiona confessed, 'so that we could move in and start using it as a holiday place right away. But Alex seems to find it conducive to work, so we may end up living here and using the Melbourne flat as a holiday place.' She paused, frowning slightly. 'You mentioned fruitwood furniture, what is that?'

'Furniture made from old fruit trees, peach, cherry trees, anything. It has a soft, mellow look, as if it has been around for a while. Just the thing for old country houses.'

'I like the sound of that, I would love to see some.'

'I have brought an old magazine with a story about it, and some pictures.' Fern dropped the thick glossy magazine she was carrying onto the existing table, as different to the kitchen furniture she had in mind as chalk from cheese. 'I'll leave that with you, so that you can study it in peace.' She turned her attention to the wood burning cooking range. 'What about that, does it heat the water?'

'Not any more!' Fiona laughed. 'When Alex discovered he was expected to grapple with that monster before he could have a shower he installed an electric immersion heater pretty damn quick.'

Fern grinned and gestured towards the new electric stove. 'I guess the same thing applied to cooking?'

'Exactly—out damn stove!' Fiona gestured theatrically in the direction of the door then looked around the kitchen thoughtfully. 'What colours have you in mind?' she asked.

'I was thinking on the lines of natural wood tones, not those earth colours, browns and greens that were so popular a while back. Something to bring the sunshine indoors. It is too dark in here, a kitchen should be light and bright, after all it's such an important room, the focal point of any house . . .' Fern stopped in mid flow, aware that she was in danger of riding her favourite hobby horse. For her this was true because she had always loved to cook. Looking around her now, she could see little evidence of cooking. Feeling a sudden pang of hunger, she remembered that she and Paul had been asked for a meal.

As if she guessed her thoughts, Fiona flashed Fern the sudden brilliant smile that won her hearts everywhere and confided, 'We brought stuff up from Melbourne, it's stacked in the fridge. What else do you plan to make this less drear?' She swept an inclusive gesture round the room.

'Get rid of those dismal Holland blinds that are stopping half the light, replace them with cheerful drapes or vertical blinds, whichever you prefer, a practical granite bench top and light fruitwood furniture for the dining area.'

'I can't wait to see it!' Fiona enthused. She moved over to the fridge. 'If you can help me put this food out we can . . .'

'Good heavens, you have enough to feed an army!' Fern exclaimed as the open door revealed shelves laden with cold chicken, smoked salmon and a variety of salads and desserts. 'Though this isn't exactly army fare.'

'Hardly,' Fiona agreed with a grin. 'Stack it on the trolley, we'll take it into the lounge. We'll dine buffet style, this kitchen looks worse than ever now you have painted such a wonderful picture of what it could be like,' she said over her shoulder as she trundled the loaded trolley in the direction of the lounge.

They had reached the coffee stage when Alex asked about her plans. Fern pushed her full coffee cup to one side and opened her folder to show him her sketches. She could feel Fiona's tense attention and when Alex finally said, 'Hmmm—I like that—I really do,' heard her breath released softly, not quite in a sigh. She remembered that Paul had told her that although Fiona would meet the bills it was Alex's approval, or otherwise, that would be the deciding factor. Odd, Fern thought, then realised there was something else odd about this evening. Though she had toured the house with Fiona there had been no sign of Beau.

'He is shut in my car,' Fiona told her when she asked about him.

'Oh, please don't banish him because of me, poor little fellow,' Fern protested. 'I don't mind him really. It's just . . .' She trailed off, wondering how to explain without sounding too utterly neurotic.

'Do you have an allergy or something?'

Fiona asked sympathetically. 'Though as poodles don't shed their hair they don't usually affect people.'

Fern shook her head. 'Yes I know, I'm not allergic to anything—as far as I know,' Fern babbled, the last thing she wanted to do was go into distressing explanations with these people she hardly knew. 'Actually I love poodles . . . you don't have to keep him shut out for me.'

Seeing the same bewilderment mirrored on all their faces she realised she would have to offer some sort of an explanation. 'It was just such a shock when I first saw him, he is so like one I had a—a while—back.' She almost succeeded in changing the tremor in her voice to a light laugh. 'I thought I was seeing a ghost, that's all.' Forcing herself to smile, she turned to Alex, 'Do you like my ideas for the kitchen?'

'Very much.' Aware of, but not understanding, her distress, he followed her lead in changing the subject. 'What plans have you for the rest of the house?'

'Nothing much as yet—if you and Fiona tell me your ideas I'll see how best to work them out.'

Fern gave Alex a wan smile, appreciating his kindness in allowing her to change the subject. Unlike Paul, she thought. But that was a little harsh. Paul really had been very kind to her, making her feel welcome and part of this new hometown.

It was after eleven when they gathered

themselves and their belongings to leave. Fern had a commission to re-do the kitchen, decorate the rest of the house and work in a second bathroom somewhere. She had also promised to arrange one of the rooms as a study/consulting room for Alex.

'I hope to spend more time here in the future,' he told her.

'Alex is writing a book,' Fiona explained.

'On psychology?' Fern asked, with a book on her own mind she was genuinely interested.

'But of course.' Alex smiled. 'Which is why I need peace and quiet, the right atmosphere, you know.'

Fern smiled back, 'I do know.'

The drive home was pleasant and uneventful, Paul keeping his chatter idle, no probing questions this time, just genuine smiles, and a lovely sparkle in his eye.

'Thank you, not just for the lift but for everything, introducing me to the Camerons and suggesting me for the job, it was good of you and I do appreciate it.' Fern was genuinely grateful and smiled at Paul with real warmth as he drew the car to a halt outside her cottage gate.

'I was doing them a favour as much as you,' he assured her. He studied her face in the ethereal light of a full moon before he switched the ignition off, slowly and deliberately.

Fern found herself returning his scrutiny.

What a nice man he was—his kindness and help had made the transfer from city living to rural life relatively painless. Now with his introduction to the Camerons he had also made it financially viable. She realised with a small shock of surprise that he was also unfathomable. She knew no more about him than the day she first met him. As always the memory of that first meeting made her pulse race. And he had almost done the same thing tonight. Thank heaven neither Alex nor Fiona seemed to notice.

Realising that she couldn't sit in Paul's car all night just looking at him as if she had lost both the will and the ability to move, Fern made an effort to collect herself. 'Would you like coffee—or anything?' seemed the polite thing to ask.

'Or anything sounds tempting.' She caught the smile as he finally opened the car door. A wave of heat flooded, not only her cheeks, but her entire body as she stepped out after him.

The pleasant company and good food and wine she had enjoyed, plus the prospect of a job she could really get her teeth into, all added to a feeling bordering on euphoria. She refused thinking room to the idea that asking Paul in at this time of night could lead to 'something'. She had made the intellectual decision that any emotional involvement was not on but she hadn't bargained for her rebellious heart and body and its response to the magnetic attraction of this man.

Paul's thoughts as he waited while she fitted her key in the lock were, had she known it, running along similar tracks. A sudden whiff of heady perfume and the nearness of her body made him acutely aware that she was a highly desirable woman. He had no more hankering for emotional entanglement than she had, but his body was sending urgent messages.

As Fern unlocked the door the cat wove between her feet and managed to slide inside as she pushed the door open. She made a half-hearted 'Tccch' of annoyance but made no effort, Paul noticed, to turn him out again. Instead she paused in her coffee making activity to pour him a generous saucer of milk. As Fern turned back to the bench, she thought how nice the evening had been and wondered at the little thrill of anticipation that ran up her spine as she thought of the prospects for the remainder of the night.

'What happened to your poodle?' he startled her by asking as she bent to place the saucer on the floor, her hand shook so that milk splashed over the edge.

'She was killed,' Fern answered tersely, just when he thought she intended to ignore his question. There was a wobble in her voice as she added, 'I'd rather not talk about it, if you don't mind.'

CHAPTER FIVE

Her hand still trembled as she set out the cups, making the china rattle in the silence. 'Do you take sugar?'

He nodded, and she wondered why she had bothered to ask. That was one of the few things she did know about him.

'Run over?'

Fern shook her head. 'I don't want to talk about it,' she repeated.

Paul shrugged. 'I'm sorry . . . I didn't mean to upset you . . .' As an apology it was clumsy, but true. He had merely tried to show an interest. He sought about in his mind for another subject to fill the lengthening silence between them.

'I was interested when you mentioned fruitwood furniture, I'd never heard of it till I saw something about it in a magazine recently.' He was relieved to see her relax at the change of topic.

'Yes—cherry wood is one of the most popular, made in either reproduction antique, often teamed with rattan, or French provincial style, it is both practical and beautiful.'

'But not cheap?' Paul guessed.

'No, not cheap,' Fern agreed. 'But well worth it if you can afford it and just perfect in an old house like the Camerons' place.'

Paul watched her face as she talked. It lost the blank closed in look it had when he had asked about her dog, and became alive so that she looked quite beautiful. He was moved, but told himself the stirring was in his loins not his heart. Putting down his empty coffee cup, he moved closer to her on the sofa.

Fern stiffened slightly, then turned to face him with a hesitant smile. It was not his fault he had touched a raw nerve when he asked about her dog, he was a nice man. The sort she would like as a friend. Nothing more. But even as her mind told her that, her body, over sensitive to his nearness, was screaming a very different message. Afterwards, Fern could not recall the moment when they came together, or even who took the first move, only the rightness of being in his arms, as if she had come home. Even in that magical moment she tried to convince herself that what she felt was nothing more than primitive physical need, it seemed an aeon since she had felt a man's arms about her, been the object of desire, or indeed known it. She sensed his need and hunger matched her own and as his fingers searched for a zip in her clothes, she pulled from him and slid to her feet, then took his hand in hers and led him to the bedroom.

Only their breathing and the sound of fingers plucking frantically at buttons and other fastenings broke the silence as they removed their own and each other's clothes and came together as smoothly and easily as a key sliding into an oiled lock. 'Aah!' his sigh synchronised perfectly with her breath being expelled on a sound that was almost a sob.

'It's been so long,' he murmured as his body relaxed and he pulled her round so that she lay facing him in the crook of his arm. Afterwards she wondered about this ambiguous remark, had he meant it personally about her or just 'so long since he'd had sex with anyone'.

'Mmm,' she murmured against his shoulder. They lay quiescent for a short while before her hand reached out to him and met his own as it began a gentle exploration of her body. His fingers moving over her bare flesh felt like electric sensors while her own discovering, or rediscovering, the contours of his body filled her with fresh waves of delight.

There was no strangeness between them, on the contrary they were like two people who knew each other so well they had no need to ask, 'Is this good?' or 'Do you enjoy that?' for their knowledge of each other's bodies was as if it were born of long intimacy. With the first sharp urgency blunted, they took their time, enjoying each other with a relaxed playfulness. Fern moved her hand across his chest, touching first one, then the other nipple with the tips of her fingers, then, with a light but firm pressure, she moved her hand, palm downward, over his stomach, rejoicing in the firm flat hardness of it. Slowly, tantalisingly, she stroked his erection with a sure but gentle touch, and then with a mischievous gurgle, she twisted her forefinger in his thick pubic hair.

With an 'ouch' of mock pain, his own hand slid between her legs, searching for the exquisitely sensitive spot he knew was there in the warm dampness. When he found it she gave a sharp cry and arched her body against his. He didn't need her soft moans to tell him that she was ready and aching for him.

When he slid inside her again the urgency had gone, he was slower, gentler, infinitely more tender. He made love to her as if he knew her intimately, and she responded in the same way. When at last they were sated and fell asleep in each other's arms, Fern's last conscious thought was that she was home—at last, safe.

*   *   *

The screaming filled the room. As Fern sat up, the sound died away and she realised with a shock that it was her own voice that had roused her. She shook her head in an attempt to clear her thoughts then buried her face in her hands. She was sweating and as she sat up the sweat turned to ice on her body so that she shook with cold as well as fear. She had been dreaming again, she knew that but was unable to recall the experience with any real clarity. All she knew was that Paul was in danger—or worse—maybe she was too late to do anything and he was already dead.

Even as she fought to remember, the dream faded, the light went on and he was sitting up in bed staring at her, the concern on his face temporarily bemused by sleep. She stared back, shaking her head once more as she tried to remember. Filled as she was with both dread and guilt maybe it was as well that full recall eluded her. Then she threw off the duvet and leapt out of bed where she stood splendid in her nakedness, quivering with repressed emotion and staring at him as if he were some sort of apparition.

'What are you doing here?' she demanded, shocking him into full wakefulness with the suddenness and apparent irrationality of the question. Surely, Paul thought, she couldn't have forgotten so soon.

'Fem . . .' He began to swing his legs over the side of the bed but she stepped back and held up one hand in a gesture that all too plainly told him to stay where he was and not come closer.

'Why are you here?' she asked again. 'You must know it is dangerous.'

Paul shrugged, totally at a loss for words as once more he cautiously swung his legs over the side of the bed, all too conscious of the fact that he, like Fern, was stark naked. He reached for his shirt, biting off the obvious retort that sprang to mind and contented himself with, 'You invited me.'

Fern stared at him, reaching automatically for her all enveloping chenille robe, wrapping it around her and pulling the cord tight with a vicious yank that made Paul wince. Fern did not appear to feel anything. 'No, no . . .' She shook her head. 'I could not have done. It would be far too dangerous.' She screwed her face up as if trying to remember. 'But if I did then it is my fault . . .' She trailed off, frowning as if puzzled.

Paul cautiously stood up, reached for the rest of his clothes, and dressed quickly. He swung round, his hand still on the zip of his fly, as her breath caught on a racking sob.

Wringing her hands in an expression of total anguish she moaned, 'You are dead because you came!'

Staring at her, Paul was shocked to see that, in spite of looking at him and pulling on her robe, she appeared to be asleep. When he realised this, he led her back to bed. He would have removed her robe but she climbed silently back between the sheets. In a few minutes she was breathing deeply.

Paul's first reaction was to leave her to her dreams, or nightmares, and drive home. The last thing he needed or wanted at this point in time was to get involved with someone with emotional hang-ups, he had enough of his own. But as he stood by the bed looking down on her, he was touched by her air of vulnerability and that curious stirring of recognition that had plagued him ever since that first meeting. Almost against his will, he lay down on the bed beside her, now fully clothed, resigned to spending the rest of the night awake. Staring at the pretty sprigged wallpaper in the soft light of the bedside lamp, he was comforted by its familiarity. Somewhere in the deepest recesses of his being, he knew that he had often lain in this room looking at this self-same pattern.

He drifted off into sleep and woke, puzzled, to find himself fully dressed in what, momentarily, was a strange room. With returning memory, he regretted the quixotic impulse that had kept him there.

Shaking his head in a vain attempt to dispel the memories of the night, Paul got slowly off the bed, feeling both uncomfortable, physically, and uneasy within himself, as if he had unwittingly got involved in some domestic fracas. But the sounds and smells that assailed him were pleasantly ordinary and domestic. A radio from the kitchen, the smell of fresh toast and percolating coffee told him that it must be breakfast time.

Fern was only half listening to the radio, wondering why they chose such bad news to start the day.

In the cold light of morning, letting Paul stay the night did not seem such a good idea. Not so much an error of judgement as weakness, permitting her body to overrule her head. It must not happen again. Emotional involvement with anything or anybody was not on her agenda right now. On this resolve she looked down at the cat, weaving round her legs demanding breakfast milk. 'As soon as you have finished breakfast—out!'

'I haven't even started breakfast yet,' Paul said from the doorway.

Fern poured a mug of coffee and passed it to him, taking in the fact that he looked slightly less rumpled than when she had left him, though he could certainly use a shave. She frowned slightly, wondering why he had been asleep on top of the bed fully clothed. 'Did you sleep—like that?' she finally asked, turning her back to drop sliced bread into the toaster.

'No, I dressed in the middle of the night.'

'In the middle of the night?' she repeated. 'Whatever for, were you leaving?'

He sipped his coffee, grateful for its strength and warmth. She looked genuinely puzzled as she waited for an explanation.

'You woke me up shouting in your sleep.'

He watched her expression change; obviously she had some recollection of the night's disturbance. The toast popped up, fracturing the silence between them.

'I . . . see.' Her voice was cool, distant. She searched her memory only to find vague disturbing dream fragments and the uncomfortable feeling that she had somehow made an awful fool of herself. 'If you found that so disturbing then why are you still here?' Fern asked, trying to control the quaver in her voice. Her back was turned to him as she put fresh bread in the toaster.

'You seemed—you were—distressed,' Paul explained, 'and I thought you were calling my name,' he foolishly added.

'How embarrassing.' Fern's attempt at flippancy was not very successful.

'For you, or for me?' His voice was dry and he looked at her directly. Fern felt herself flush. 'I was probably mistaken,' he added soothingly, his lips curving in a gentle smile as he reached for the toast. 'You did seem pretty distressed though.'

'Well, I'm not now,' Fern snapped, wishing he would just shut up and stop harping on the night they had spent together. 'Anyway it was only a dream.'

'About me?' he persisted. 'Actually, you seemed to think I was dead. Will you tell me about it?'

'No—I can't remember it very well—it's just a silly recurring dream.'

'Are you telling me you often dream of me?' Paul's slightly amused smile infuriated her.

'No, of course not, and anyway, if I did, it is my dream. It isn't important, so stop making a big deal out of it because you think you heard me yell out your name in the night. Dreaming about you doesn't give you copyright over my dreams.' Fern knew she was protesting far too vigorously, but it seemed, once started, she couldn't stop. 'Look—like I said, my dreams are my dreams, I'm sorry if I woke you. Maybe you shouldn't have stayed last night.'

'Maybe I shouldn't,' Paul shrugged, in an attempt to hide the curiosity, aroused by her obvious reluctance to share with him the contents of her dream. Against all logic he felt that he had a right to know.

His seeming indifference and casual agreement sparked off righteous indignation in Fern, fuelled by her anxiety about what had really happened in the night. 'Too right!' she retorted, 'and I don't think you should come again, I've had more than enough of your— your nonsense.' Why couldn't she think of a better word than that? 'First you make out you know me from God knows where, then you sell me a haunted house, then . . .'

Paul held up his hand and interrupted her. 'Hold on a minute, what do you mean, haunted?'

What did she mean? Fern was at a loss how to answer. 'Well, ever since I've been here I have had these odd dreams as if . . .' but she couldn't explain to him that the house and Paul himself were always curiously mixed up in her dreams.

'Are you telling me that you think the house is haunted because you dream in it? You never dreamed before I suppose?'

'Of course I did.' Fern thought of the terrifying nightmares she had experienced. 'But I knew where they came from, they . . . they were an extension of my daily life. These are bizarre, and I don't want them any more— so keep away.'

Paul stood up abruptly, trying to hold back the furious retorts that rose to his lips.

'Willingly!' he assured her, his voice cold.

He felt tired and out of sorts, in no fit state to face a day's work. God, he needed a shower and a shave at least before he fronted up at the office. At the door he turned to her. 'You *bought* this house,' he pointed out. 'I didn't *sell* it to you against your will. You came to me for professional help.' He snatched open the door, then turned back once more. 'Thanks for the coffee anyway.' His tone was grudging, suggesting that was all he had to thank her for.

Fern knew she deserved that, even so the door closing, none too gently, behind Paul felt like a physical blow. She might have felt better if a sharp and witty retort had flashed from her lips but her mind remained blank and her tongue still.

'Well, that's the end of a promising beginning.' If only it was possible to turn the clocks back and re-run the events of the previous evening. But the best she could do was try and put it and everything to do with Paul Denton behind her. And the way to do that, Fern knew, was work.

She didn't need the breakfast dishes sitting there as a silent reminder. She cleared them away as quickly as possible. Once done, she turned to her laptop, her sketches, swatches of fabric and paint colour charts, and directed all her attention to creating the perfect country kitchen for Fiona and Alex Cameron.

She knew she was lucky in her clients, they seemed to have enthusiasm and good taste and the means to carry out their ideas. This commission could be the start of her country business. She tried to forget that she owed this important introduction to Paul.

With a great deal of effort and will, she pushed all thoughts of dreams, nightmares—and Paul—to the back of her mind. Work was what she needed, the perfect antidote to lift her spirits.

By lunchtime she had redesigned the kitchen to her satisfaction and after a scratch meal of coffee and cheese sandwiches she started a piece on the latest trends in bathrooms for one of the interior decorating glossies that she wrote for.

By the time that was finished she was hungry again but also felt headachy and housebound. Fleetingly she wished for a dog to give her a reason to walk outdoors. As quickly as the thought came she repulsed it. Her own feelings were enough to take her out of the house and she was no more ready to open her heart to another dog than she could to another man.

A spring breeze seemed to be rising, she could hear it breathing and sighing around the old house. She pulled on a light parka and set off, relishing the feel of the wind against her cheeks and enjoying the way it whipped at her hair.

Half an hour later she was back in the cottage, refreshed and revived, almost revitalised. She looked with some satisfaction at the work she had achieved that day. The kitchen design looked even better when she revisited it. Impulsively, she picked up the phone and called Fiona. It was Alex who answered.

'Oh,' Fern said, confused. Why should she be surprised, after all, he also lived at the number she had called, and was probably there a good deal more than Fiona.

'Oh,' she repeated, feeling foolish. 'I thought Fiona might like to see the plans for the kitchen, I've just completed them.'

'She's away off to Melbourne. Getting ready to go on tour,' Alex told her, 'but why don't I look at them? I was just about to come into town anyway so I'll be with you shortly.'

Fern replaced the receiver slowly. She didn't know whether or not Alex had heard her murmured, 'Fine—I'll see you,' or whether his receiver going down had cut off the words. She flicked the jug on, a cup of tea would not come amiss, and waited for him.

Twenty minutes later he was sitting opposite her drinking tea and looking at the plans. Fern, her cup clasped between both hands, watched him over the rim and tried to guess his reactions. She reminded herself that it was Fiona who was paying her and who she had to please, but somewhere inside her head was an echo of Paul's voice warning her that it was important that Alex liked them.

He put his cup down and looked at her. 'Say, these are just great!'

'Do you think Fiona will be happy with them?' Fern asked.

'She'll be ecstatic, get the work under way as quickly as you can.'

'Shouldn't I wait till she has seen them?' Fern asked anxiously. 'After all . . .' she bit off the words feeling it might not be tactful to remind Alex that it was Fiona who would foot the bill.

'She will be more than happy, I can assure you, and delighted to get back and find all the work done.'

'She isn't coming back till her tour ends?'

'I doubt it—she won't have time, so—if you can get the ball rolling . . .'

'If you say so.' Fern still felt doubtful, but it would be good to get it done and be able to add the after photos to her folio. 'About the furniture, do you want me to go ahead and get that as well?' she asked.

'But of course, do the whole thing, I'll leave a key with Paul, the place will be empty. I shall be in Melbourne for a week or two as I have appointments. When I come back I want to get some work done on my book.'

Interested, Fern asked, 'What is the subject of your book?'

'Dreams, hypnosis, regression, back even to past lives, I'm interested in the connection.'

'You think there is one?' Fern asked dryly. 'Aren't dreams just the random wanderings of the brain when we are unconscious?'

'I don't think so,' Alex told her. 'Far from it in fact, you must dream yourself and have often thought there was more to them than that.'

'I don't dream,' she told him shortly, pushing her chair away from the table and gathering up their cups.

'Everyone dreams, but not everyone remembers, or wants to remember,' Alex said emphatically, warming to his subject.

Fern, with her back to him, concentrated on rinsing the cups they had used and chose to ignore him. She had no intention of getting bogged down in a discussion on dreams with a clinical psychologist who would certainly have the edge on her. Even less of discussing her own dreams and becoming one of Alex's interesting subjects. For a fleeting moment she wondered if Paul had mentioned anything about her to him but when she turned round and faced him she was relieved to find that he was once more studying her plans for their kitchen.

'Could you get most of this done while I am away? Or is that . . .' he added seeing the incredulity on her face, 'rather a tall order?'

'It is,' she told him. 'How far I get very much depends on other people.'

'Well—do your best.' He got up from the table in one graceful movement. Watching him, she once more registered his startling good looks but he did not attract her in the least. There was a lack of spontaneity and warmth about him that she found chilling, the very opposite of Fiona who bubbled over with those qualities. She was wondering what had attracted them to each other when his next remark stunned her.

'My sister will be away for six weeks, so you shouldn't have any problem getting it done before she gets back. Thanks for the tea.'

Fern was still absorbing this information when she heard his car drive away. Why hadn't Paul told her they were brother and sister not husband and wife? But then, she admitted honestly to herself, he hadn't actually said that either, just always referred to them as 'The Camerons' or Alex and Fiona. Fern was seared by an emotion that, if she had allowed herself to consider, she might have identified as jealousy as she wondered about the nature of the relationship between Paul and Fiona.

It took all her strength of mind to dismiss the Camerons and Paul from her mind and concentrate on her work. What happened last night had just been one of those things and as far as she was concerned it certainly would never happen again. She wished it were not necessary to see Paul and collect the key of the Camerons' house. Maybe she could avoid actually seeing him. She intended using the same builder who had done her renovations and had all the necessary contact details.

She was at Paul's office before he arrived. He had left instructions with Dot that Fern was to be given the key.

She was already in her car when he drove up.

When he saw her, he leapt out of his own car and hurried over. Feeling obliged to do so, Fern wound down the window. 'Hi,' she held up the key in explanation. 'Thanks,' she added with a brief smile before she touched the accelerator, released the handbrake and drove off. Her rear-view mirror revealed him looking after her with a bemused expression. Fern tried to convince herself that she was relieved, but a strangle tingle of regret dented her resolve.

Fern immersed herself in the Camerons' kitchen. By wanting it completed in such a short time frame Alex had thrown her a challenge. But it was such a good commission with the promise of more to come that she

105

enjoyed meeting it. Most nights she was tired enough to fall quickly asleep but that didn't always stop her dreaming. Nor could she dismiss Paul from her thoughts for he had a remarkable facility for appearing at the same places that she did, the only consolation was that these thoughts and her work were keeping other thoughts, memories of Nigel and the reason why she was here at all, at bay. She kept her phone almost permanently on the answering service.

She forgot that she had given Paul her mobile number until the phone bleeped in her pocket as she stood in Fiona's re-designed kitchen contemplating the new fruitwood table and dresser that had just been delivered.

'You are hard to reach!' were his first words when she answered.

'Am I?' She tried to still the thumping of her heart and ignore the breathless feeling that overcame her. Fern was not to know that Paul had been fighting a losing battle with himself to refrain from calling her, each time he passed a phone or his hand strayed towards his mobile the temptation was there. He finally succumbed, telling himself that he needed to be in contact with her for business reasons. Neither was she to know that he was every bit as opposed to 'getting involved' as she was.

'I just wondered how things were going,' Paul tried to sound casual.

'Fine, fine, it looks just great. In fact I was

just standing here admiring it when you rang.'

'Why don't I come and admire it with you?'

'Yes, why don't you?' The pause was just long enough for him to wonder if he had overstepped the mark. 'But I was just about to leave.'

'I'm on the way!' He was, in fact, halfway there when he called her. Even so, the workmen had cleared up their stuff and left and Fern was just walking out onto the verandah.

Paul jumped quickly out of his car and then, slowing himself down deliberately, strolled across to her.

Fern stood still, watching him. 'Hi, that didn't take long!'

He grinned. 'I'll be honest; I was actually on the way when I rang. Lead on, I'm really keen to see what you have made of that old kitchen.'

'I'll bet you are!' Fern turned as she led the way into the house. 'Your reputation as well as mine hangs on it after the recommendation you gave me for the job.'

'It was what you have done to your own place as much as anything I said that got you the deal,' Paul told her. He paused in the kitchen doorway. 'Wow!' he let out his breath in a whistle, his eyes roaming around the refurbished room.

'But this is terrific, far better than I fancied it, I love this stuff.' He ran his hand over the wood of the dresser as if he were stroking a living creature. 'Is this the fruit wood you were talking about?'

Fern nodded, she didn't trust herself to speak without betraying how much his approval meant to her. Her glance drifted round the room, now totally transformed and utterly her own creation, before finding her voice. 'Yes, that's cherry wood. Lovely isn't it?'

'Absolutely beautiful,' Paul agreed, but his eyes were on Fern, not the dresser.

'Do you think the Camerons will like it?' Fern frowned slightly as her eyes travelled the room. Always critical of her own work she could find no fault with this job. The dreary, inconvenient kitchen had been transformed into a light and ultra convenient area designed for the preparation and consumption of good food.

'I've been taking "after" photos,' she confessed to Paul. 'When I look at my "before" ones I can hardly believe that it is the same mom. Yet some of the structural changes were actually so simple, like having everything on the same side, stove, sink etc. 'She turned to him now and asked, 'Do you like this dining setting, more important do you think Fiona will?' She indicated a soft honey-coloured oval dining table with eight rush seated ladder-backed chairs round it. 'Peachwood,' she told him.

'Of course they will!' Paul assured her. 'You've made an absolutely terrific job of it.

Are you going to do the rest of the house?'

'I think so, I hope so anyway, but I guess I will have to have some more consultations with Fiona. Do you know when she is due back?'

'Next week, as far as I know.'

'Oh.' Fern caught her breath. How did he know, were he and Fiona in communication? Unconsciously she retaliated. 'Alex told me he would only be away for a couple of weeks but I haven't seen or heard from him.'

'He'll be up here,' Paul assured her. 'I expect you are eager to show it to them both now?'

'Well—yes,' Fern admitted. 'It seems a bit flat having no-one to show it to, except you.'

Paul empathised with her and said impulsively, 'I think this calls for a celebration, how about dinner tonight?'

'Thank you, that would be nice.' Fern was surprised to hear herself accept but beans on toast by herself was not an exciting alternative.

Paul helped her lock up before they left and promised to pick her up around seven that evening. As she drove back home, Fern felt happier than she had for a long time, she was satisfied with the work she had done and pleased to be working again. She let herself and the cat into her cottage and looked around it with pleasure, it was becoming home and she knew she had done a good job here too. She hummed to herself as she made her way to the shower.

The feeling of euphoria and pleasant anticipation was still with her as she dressed and sat down in front of the mirror. This in itself was one of her minor triumphs. She had found it in the old bathroom, now demolished. It was filthy and the mirror itself hung crookedly as it was missing a screw on one side. It had an adjustable tilt and the base, on four round feet, had two small drawers. Miraculously the glass itself was unharmed. Tender loving care had turned it into a beautiful little piece, probably of some value. She used it on top of a small table instead of a dressing table. She was staring into it now, leaning forward slightly, as she concentrated on applying her eye make-up. Thinking the glass must be steaming up with her own breath she rubbed it with a tissue, but it failed to clear the mist that in the most odd way seemed to be coming from inside the mirror itself.

Fern stared harder and as she did so her face swam into focus, only it wasn't her face—was it?

She was still wearing a garment of rich plum colour, but the fabric itself seemed to have changed from crisp matt cotton to a shiny watered silk. The collar too had grown, it now stood up to her ears and was edged with rich cream lace, beneath it the décolleté neckline of her dress revealed the cleft between her breasts, she was wearing jewellery, a necklace and matching pendant earrings. Her face was free of make-up, but her hair was beautifully and elaborately dressed. Behind her, clearly visible over her right shoulder, was another face, again easily recognisable as Paul even though he, too, wore a garment with a stiff high white ruff around his neck. He had a small pointed black beard and his hands were resting lightly on her shoulders.

Even as she watched his face faded, her own features once more wavered and swam, the mist swirled in the glass and cleared and she saw herself, hand poised with a mascara brush between her fingers, putting the final touches to her make-up.

Fern shook her head as if to rid herself of the vision, mirage, dream, figment of her imagination, she truly did not know into which category the experience fitted. Or even if she had experienced it at all. With a determined effort of will she dismissed the whole thing as imagination and concentrated wholly on the task in hand, making up her face, but her hand shook making it difficult.

While she was convinced that she had indeed succeeded in dismissing the whole foolish incident from her mind, nevertheless she found she was covertly studying Paul's features across the dinner table. She had made her own selection swiftly from the menu and when she looked up he was still intent on making a choice, it gave her a chance to watch him without him being aware of it.

Fern smiled softly to herself, he had looked good with the Elizabethan ruff round his neck and the neat beard also did something for him. He had, she decided, quite a medieval face.

He looked up then and smiled at her over the single candle that flickered in the middle of the table. Management's bid for a romantic ambience.

'Have I got a large black smudge on my nose, showing that five o'clock shadow on my chin or are you just committing my face to memory for future reference?'

'I'm sorry, Paul, I didn't mean to stare, it is just that you suddenly reminded me of someone in an oil painting,' she hastily extemporised.

'I hope he was a handsome guy? I must say I never thought of myself as any oil painting!'

'I didn't say you were, just that you reminded me of someone in a picture.' Fern matched his light bantering tone. She nearly told him that it was in a mirror, not a gilt frame that she had seen him, but he might think she had quite lost her marbles.

They remained in this light-hearted frame of mind throughout the evening. It was a long time since either of them had enjoyed the company of someone of the opposite sex so much. Fern too still felt a glow of satisfaction that only creative achievement can bestow.

'Thank you, Paul, for putting this job my

way.' She reached out across the table and impulsively touched his hand. 'It has really got me back into harness.' She smiled deprecatingly. 'Not a good expression, I really enjoy my work, it would have been more accurate to say I am back on the carousel.'

'I think I did Alex and Fiona a favour, they think so too,' he assured her.

After a leisurely meal Paul took Fern back to the cottage, it seemed churlish not to ask him in. 'Thank you, Paul, for a lovely evening.' She stretched and yawned, pleasantly tired and feeling relaxed and at ease. 'Will you stay for a nightcap?'

He raised an eyebrow, he had been hoping for more than that. 'Thanks,' he said and followed her in.

'What would you like, whisky, beer, wine, coffee, tea or—cocoa?'

'Did you say cocoa?' Paul's expression reminded her of the cat when she picked the can-opener up out of the kitchen drawer, 'and if so were you serious?'

'I did say cocoa, and I was being facetious, but I do have some if you would really rather have that than anything?'

'I would—but not "than anything,"' the last under his breath. 'It is years since I had cocoa before I went to bed.' He went to the cupboard and pulled out two mugs as if it were the usual thing for him to do. Fern knew he hoped to stay the night, she also knew that, in spite of all her resolve, she would let him. Seduced, she thought, by the cosy intimacy of cocoa for two.

There was no doubt sipping hot chocolate together did engender a warm togetherness. It was a long time since Fern had been so relaxed, she smiled at Paul and felt her heart skip a beat as his eyes met hers and their glance held for a second.

'I can stay, Fern?' His voice was husky with desire.

CHAPTER SIX

'No—No!' her mind screamed, but her treacherous body cried 'Yes' though it was in a voice little more than a whisper, that she spoke the word aloud. What had happened to her 'Never again' resolve? She would have been surprised to know that Paul was asking himself the same question.

Fern felt the silence hum as they looked at one another, simultaneously they placed their empty mugs down. Then Paul reached for her hand across the table. 'Come.' The single word was spoken softly but there was an urgency in his voice that set Fern's blood singing. Without speaking, she took his hand and together they left the kitchen.

In spite of their throbbing hunger for each

other, there was no feverish haste this time. On the contrary, they undressed each other slowly, taking it in turns to remove a garment and savouring to the hilt their pleasure in their own and each other's bodies. Their lack of speed added sensuality to their movements and became a powerful form of foreplay. We have, Fern mused, all the time in the world. But when he reached for her panties, the last garment to remove, and she felt his fingers on her bare skin, a ripple of desire shimmied up her spine and she flung herself in his arms, pressing her body against his, glorying in his hardness.

He pushed her back into the pillows pulling off her panties with less than his former gentleness. She wouldn't have objected if he had literally torn them off her. Never, in her whole life, had she felt such hunger for any man, nor had anyone given her such deep satisfaction as Paul. They were so perfectly attuned to each other, yet she hardly knew him. She stopped thinking and gave her entire self up to feeling.

She was lying, utterly relaxed, in the crook of his arm, her head resting on his shoulder, not quite sure whether she was awake or asleep, when she felt, rather than heard, him sigh. With an effort she opened one eye and looked at his face, so close to her own. A faint frown drew his brows together and she opened the other eye to see him better. 'What is it?'

she asked, suddenly concerned. Had she failed to please him in some way?

He didn't move his head but went on staring straight ahead at the wall. 'It's that damn wallpaper,' he admitted at last. 'I just can't get over the feeling that I have gone to sleep looking at it and woken to see it again—and again. Yet for the life of me I can't remember it being in any house I've ever lived in . . .' his voice trailed off, the words 'in this life' left unsaid. Fern had taken him to task before for his odd behaviour, he didn't want her to think he was a total nutter.

'Perhaps it was in another life,' Fern suggested, tongue in cheek, but he failed to hear—or chose to ignore—the sarcasm in her voice.

He turned to her with a pleased smile. 'Yes, that must be it, that's probably why you chose it—you remembered it too.'

Fern stiffened slightly in his arms. 'I chose it because it seemed the right thing to do when I found it was available. I was restoring the place, remember, and what could bring it back to its original state better than the same wallpaper. That was absolutely the only reason I put it on. Plus, of course, I really liked it, if I hadn't I wouldn't have chosen it, I can assure you. I wish I had picked something else if it is going to give you such batty ideas.'

'I'm sorry.' The tone of his voice made it clear he didn't think there was anything to be sorry about, and if there was—he wasn't. Fern, afraid they were on the verge of repeating the quarrel that had separated them before, bit off a facetious comment about reincarnation and moved her hand gently down his body till it encircled his penis, her touch bringing it to life. Paul rolled over on top of her, wallpaper forgotten, in the urgency of his need for her.

But later, when he looked at her sleeping face, pale and vulnerable in the light of a full moon, he felt again that disturbing stab of recognition. He wondered what tragic events from her past disturbed her dreams and wondered still more what part their meeting seemed to play in reliving these. If only he had the capacity to make them go away. But he understood only too well how hard they could be to overcome.

*   *   *

Fern was once again in that disturbing dream in which she was forced to look down from a balcony on her lover's body. It was always the same, always she caught a glimpse of the ringed finger before his face was revealed. She never seemed to know quite what had happened, only that in some way it was because of her, because he loved her, and she him and one—or both—of them had been indiscreet. Horror engulfed her, he was dead, he was her lover, her other half, her soul mate

117

and he was dead.

She put up a hand to stifle the howl of pain that she could feel rising within and fighting for release and as she did so, noticed the rich stiff silk of her dress in a deep magenta colour with ruffles at the wrist. She felt, rather than saw, the woman at her side and slightly behind her and knew that though she was her servant she was also her friend. She felt the warning in the light touch on her arm.

She was standing on a balcony, a flat area in the wide staircase about halfway up its flight. There was a polished wooden rail in front of her, the handrail of the banisters: she gripped it with her free hand so hard the knuckles shone white. As her grip tightened on the wood she slowly lowered her other hand from her mouth and raised her eyes from the much-loved face to that of the man standing by the bier. The cruel lines etched round his mouth curved into a slight smile of triumph. Their eyes locked, then he bowed sardonically, and she turned away. As she walked to her own rooms she managed to keep her back straight and her step measured, inside she was screaming, howling, sobbing, and drowning in the huge wave of grief and loss that threatened to destroy her. She felt someone take her arm and shake her. 'Come—Mistress . . .' the woman was saying, kindness softening the rough country burr, her grip tightening on her arm in both warning and support.

She tried to shake her arm free of the vice-like

grip it seemed to be held in.

'Leave me be!' She thought she sounded imperious and in command, but her voice came out as a pathetic quaver. 'Leave me alone.' She half-turned as she spoke, then with a shuddering moan she felt her knees buckle.

'Paul?' she whispered and tried to sit up, but a dizzying pain shot through her head and she flopped back again on the pillows.

'Don't try to sit up,' his hand, firm and gentle held her down. 'You had a bad dream, you must have been sleep-walking. You keeled over and hit your head on the corner of the bed. You will probably have a bruise there tomorrow, stay there and I'll find something to put on it.'

She closed her eyes and lay still, realising that he must have picked her up bodily and placed her back on the bed. When she felt something blissfully cool on her temple and smelt the fresh smell, she knew he must have found the witch hazel. 'Gran treated all my bumps and bruises with that, so I always keep a bottle handy,' she murmured.

'Good stuff,' Paul agreed, the sweet coolness had brought back his own childhood memories as he gently applied it to the darkening bump on her temple.

'You were screaming blue murder, I thought we had an intruder.'

Fern almost wished that they had. Tonight's experience had left her shaken to the core. She felt that she had lived the experience, not dreamed it.

'Is this a regular occurrence, or something I trigger?'

'I don't have these dreams often, but yes— this particular one you do seem to trigger off.' Her own weakness and his caring, gentle tone made it impossible to dissemble.

'Have you any idea why?'

'None at all, unless . . .' She trailed off, unwilling to admit the possibility of some previous connection. But she had not forgotten the curious intimacy of that moment when he tilted her chin and she looked into his eyes.

'I know you will think this bizarre,' he looked embarrassed, 'but there seems a connection between my thinking that we had met before and your dreams.'

Startled, Fern looked up into his face. Was he reading her thoughts? Of course not, just coincidence. She closed her eyes and listened to him returning the witch hazel to the bathroom.

They flew open when he came back to the bed and asked, 'Do you believe in reincarnation?'

Fern stared at him, her first reaction that he was joking, surely no-one believed in that fanciful nonsense?

'You mean do I think I was Anne Boleyn in my last life and I might be a cat in the next?'

Hearing the facetious note in her voice she felt slightly ashamed. He had asked the question in good faith.

'I'm sorry, I was being flippant,' Fern hastened to apologise. 'Please explain what you mean exactly. Reincarnation is a subject I am rather hazy on. I thought it was something only weirdos believed in.'

'If you put more than half the population of the world into that category, including me, then you are right.' Fern thought he had closed the subject as he settled back in the bed but it seemed he was merely searching for convincing words. 'Do you believe that you have something beside a body?'

Fern did her best to answer truthfully. 'I think there is something, I'm not sure what, perhaps I would describe it as the essence of a person, some thing that makes you, you and me, me. I suppose that is what religious people mean when they talk about the soul.' Fern shrugged. 'I am not putting this very well at all, but, yes—I suppose my answer is yes, in a broad sense, I do.'

'And what do you think happens to that—essence—when you die?' Paul probed.

'If pushed, I would have to say that I hope, and would like to believe, that it survived. I'm self centred enough not to relish the thought of just fizzling out into nothingness at the end,' Fern admitted.

'And what about before you began, do you

think that essence or whatever only came into existence the day you were born?'

'Hell, Paul. I can't say, I have never given it much thought.'

'Well, think now.' He gave her a small smile of encouragement, softening his direct approach.

'Well, I suppose it is only logical that if that part of a person survives the physical death of the body, then it could also be around before the body?'

'Around—where?' Paul persisted.

'In some other body?' Fern suggested. 'And that, you are now going to tell me, is reincarnation and I have just admitted to subscribing to the belief.'

'You got it!' Dropping his inquisitorial manner, Paul grinned, reached for her hand beneath the bedclothes, and pulled her gently but firmly towards him.

'Perhaps . . .' Fern was thoughtful, 'my nightmares are a hangover from another life. I thought they arose from traumas and events in this one. Even garbled rehash of stuff in my brain, perhaps something I've read, or a film I've seen.'

She glanced at the clock. 'Paul, it's nearly two a.m.,' she pointed out. 'We should go back to sleep if we want to have any hope of being bright eyed and bushy tailed in the morning.' She gently removed his straying hand from her body before he aroused her again. Her head throbbed, whether from the bump or the effort of thinking, she wasn't sure, but sleep seemed a real imperative right now.

'I guess you are right,' he muttered. As he turned off the light, Fern sighed and moved closer into the curve of his body.

She woke to a strong smell of coffee and the feel of something thumping down on the bed. The two, she saw as she forced open heavy eyes, were connected. Paul had brought her breakfast in bed. She looked at the tray, laid with toast and coffee for one. 'Aren't you . . .'

Paul shook his head. 'I had a quick one downstairs, I thought you needed your sleep.' He rubbed his hand ruefully over his chin, dark with stubble. 'I must get home and make myself presentable.'

'Mmmm, I suppose so,' Fern murmured, uncomfortably aware that as far as that went she must look far worse. Ungratefully she wished he had just left her sleeping. At least then she wouldn't have had to face him with the embarrassing memory of once more making an utter idiot of herself, as she was sure she had done again the previous night. Twice must surely be enough, he would not be back for more.

She drank her coffee strong and black then headed for the shower. She winced as her fingers inadvertently touched the bruise on her temple, but felt more like herself and even ready to face the day as she towelled herself dry. She liked Paul—really liked him, as a person. Not just because they had great sex together. What was more, she even liked herself when she was with him, but it was humiliating to wake screaming every time they slept together. Maybe he was the trigger that set her off.

The only way to find that out would be not to sleep with him again.

She found this line of thought depressing and, determined to put both Paul and her wretched dreams into perspective, she took herself off to the Cameron place to check the workmen had left everything in order. Alex was due home today and Fiona in a couple of days' time. Looking around the newly furbished kitchen she felt warmed and reassured. It looked great, even better than she had visualised. There was no satisfaction, she decided, to equal that of a creative job well done. The insistent bleep of her mobile phone cut short her self-congratulation.

'Oh, hello Alex.' Fern crushed the shaft of regret that it was not Paul, forgetting that only seconds before she had felt that work satisfaction was the greatest thing in life. 'The kitchen is finished and all ready to use, when does Fiona get back?' she asked. 'I do hope she likes it.'

'Not till the end of the week, but I am coming home today. I want to get on with my book, there are too many distractions here. I will have a few days' total peace before Fiona arrives.'

'I'm at your place at the moment, Alex, just giving it a final check, making sure the decorators had cleared up properly, but I am just off, so you will have it to yourself. Do you want me to leave the key here for you, and if so, where?'

'Can you stay? I shall be there shortly, I am not far away. I really would appreciate it if you could hang on.'

'Oh, all right, I'll be here then,' Fern agreed.

'See you in a few minutes . . . I have Beau with me.' He added this as if as an afterthought. Warning her, Fern guessed, embarrassed by the memory of her reaction when she had first seen the dog.

Alex must have been very close, or have driven like the wind for, barely seconds later, she heard his car draw up outside. She watched from the window as he let the excited little poodle out then, bracing herself to face them both, she walked to the door to meet him. She led the way straight to the kitchen.

'Wow! I really like this, it's a total transformation!' he exclaimed.

'That was the idea.' Fern smiled, glowing with pleasure at his praise. 'Even though I say it myself, it does look good. But do you think Fiona will like it?'

'She will be over the moon, I'm sure. It might even inspire her to cook. As soon as she gets back you must come for a meal and bring your ideas for the rest of the house. Perhaps Paul could come too.'

'Yes, perhaps he could.' Fern looked him coolly in the eye hoping the warm feeling in her cheeks was imagination. She pulled her car keys out of her pocket and tossed them in her hand, suddenly anxious to be off. Alex was making her uncomfortable, although he had been nothing but charming. Was it because she now knew him as Fiona's brother? But that, she told herself, was childish. The gesture with the car keys was not lost on Alex.

'I won't keep you any longer,' he told her. Then as she turned for the door, he added, 'I saw you mentioned in one of the glossies the other day, "House Beautiful" or something, then coincidentally I read a piece by you in another magazine. It seems you are quite somebody in the world of interior design.'

Fern shrugged deprecatingly. What could she say, 'Oh yes, I'm a real hotshot?' Equally absurd to deny her success. She smiled and turned to leave, but Alex had not finished.

'The piece about you hinted at some dark trauma in your past. I must admit I had wondered why someone so well-known in the city should be living here in the bush doing up old farmhouses.'

Anger flared, swift and sudden, manifesting itself in the rush of colour to her cheeks. She bit off a sharp retort that it was no damn business of his, and with a supreme effort smiled as sweetly as she could and retorted in kind. 'I was wondering much the same thing, why would a successful psychologist and a well-known Country and Western singer buy an old farmhouse and live here. Bye Alex.' She turned swiftly on her heel and walked to her car with as much speed and dignity as she could muster, leaving Alex aghast in her wake.

Fern was almost home before her anger abated and she paused to ask herself just what had made her so cross. She couldn't, in all honesty, blame Alex, who had been pleasant, even complimentary. Was she afraid of having to face up to her past, or of Alex seeing behind the new persona she had built up for herself?

By the time she arrived at her own cottage she had convinced herself that she had merely over-reacted to what was probably a totally well-meant comment. She flopped down in her most comfortable armchair, leaned back with a sigh and within minutes was fast asleep.

She woke an hour or so later with a stiff neck and a feeling of disorientation, as she often did when she dropped off during the day, she was not a good cat-napper. She had a vague sense of having dreamed but could not recall the content, the crick in her neck was because her head had dropped forward and sideways as she slept. Still feeling muzzy, she headed for the kitchen, the electric jug, and a reviving cuppa.

She heard a car door slamming shut as she poured boiling water over a teabag. Craning to look through the window she watched Paul walk to the door. Still fuddled by sleep, she combed her fingers through her hair before she opened the door.

'Hi, could you use a cup of tea?'

'Could I ever! I have spent the entire day showing houses to people who don't seem to have the faintest idea what they really want, only that it needs to be different to the one I am showing them.'

He sat down in the chair opposite her with a sigh and thankfully accepted the cup she passed to him. 'You look a bit washed out yourself,' he told her with less than flattering truthfulness.

'Oh, thanks, you've made my day.' Fern's voice was acid. 'Well, for the record, my day hasn't been too bad, I've been showing Alex the new kitchen.'

'And, was he pleased?'

'I think so, very. Well, he seemed to be anyway and he thought Fiona would be delighted with it when she gets back from her tour.'

'Great, you should be on top of the world.' Then, as if remembering, 'It must be the after effects of the dream you had.' He stared at her over the rim of his teacup. 'Would you like to talk about it?'

For a moment she was tempted, what a

relief it might be to simply pour it all out and transfer the burden to someone else. But not Paul, he was far too intimately involved. 'No thanks.' Her tone was short.

Paul shrugged. 'Just as you like, I thought . . .' his voice faded. There seemed little sense in pursuing the matter if she refused to talk, whatever his own opinion.

Fern shook her head. 'I—I can't really remember anyway.'

Paul shrugged again, that rather Gallic shrug that had touched a hidden memory and made him seem almost as familiar to her as she to him at their first meeting. He turned away from her and, watching his lips tighten, Fern knew she had hurt him. She was sorry, but she couldn't talk to him about the dream, it was too embarrassing to recount his involvement and also too painful to invoke the memory of Nigel and the feelings engendered by memories of her life with him.

After a few minutes he put his empty cup back in the saucer, and stood up. 'I'd better push off, I still have a lot of bookwork to do. Thanks for the tea, I must say it takes some beating as a quick restorative.' With a brief smile he was gone, leaving her with a feeling of failure; she had handled things badly.

As the door closed behind him Fern determined she would put all thoughts other than the satisfaction of having done a creative job well, out of her head. For once she would just relish the independence she had achieved, and enjoy being her own person in her own home. For the remainder of the day she pottered in the little garden, fed the cat, prepared a simple meal for herself and ate it in a relaxed state in front of the T.V. She went up to bed early, read for a while then dropped off into a deep dreamless sleep, or at least one in which she was not aware of dreaming.

Two days later, she had a phone call from Fiona, breathless with excitement. 'I just love my new kitchen, it is positively awesome; the fruitwood furniture is beautiful, it looks so right in there. You are brilliant, you've turned a disaster area into a fantastic kitchen anyone would adore to work in.' She paused for breath, laughter rippling through her words. 'Pity my culinary skill only runs to boiling the jug, making toast, and using the microwave, but I'm tempted.' Fern heard her take another quick breath before rushing on. 'What about the rest of the house, when can you come and tell me what marvellous ideas you have for that?'

Fern glanced at her watch, it was still only mid morning. 'Now?' Then remembering that Fiona herself had only just got back from her tour, 'That is if you are not too tired. How was the tour, a great success, I bet.'

'Terrific, absolutely fabulous.' Fern was getting used to Fiona's way of talking in superlatives. 'And now would be great, I'll be waiting. See you!'

Quickly gathering up designs, colour charts and some odd swatches of fabric, Fern was on her way.

Fern drew the car to a halt in the shade of the trees and almost before she had switched off the ignition, Fiona burst out of the house, accompanied by Beau, excited to be reunited with his mistress, who chose to ignore Fern's attitude towards him. She ran forward with a wide smile.

'Hey, you look loaded, let me take some,' Fiona exclaimed as she relieved Fern of a wad of magazines and a folder. 'Coffee is on and Alex out, foraging for lunch, so it's just us.' She led Fern into the kitchen. 'Look, isn't it wonderful?' she exclaimed as if Fern had never seen it before.

Over coffee Fern outlined her ideas for the rest of the house and together they pored over colour charts and fingered the fabric swatches. They were startled to hear car doors slamming and male voices some three-quarters of an hour later.

Fiona jumped up and went to the window. 'Oh, lovely, Alex has brought Paul back with him.'

At her words, Fern suddenly became all thumbs as she started to gather her belongings. 'I'll be getting along now.' She tried to sound casual. 'I have enough ideas to work on, I'll call you when I have something on paper.'

'Don't go, stay for lunch—please.' Fiona put her hand on Fern's arm as if to physically detain her. Before she had time to either refuse or acquiesce, the two men were in the room. Fiona leapt to her feet to greet Paul with what seemed, to Fern, overdone spontaneous delight. She turned away and caught a flash of annoyance that seemed to mirror her own feelings, flit across Alex's face. She might have thought she was imagining it had she not also caught the anxious, almost fearful, glance Fiona threw at her brother. There seemed to be undercurrents here she did not understand, any more than she did the turmoil of her own feelings at seeing Paul again. She would not admit to feeling jealous when, after greeting Fiona warmly with a kiss, even if it was brotherly, Paul turned to her with the briefest nod and a curt, 'Hi, Fern.'

Alex was in the kitchen unpacking his shopping, the sound of fridge and pantry doors opening and closing punctuated the background of plastic bags being emptied to the accompaniment of Alex humming, not very tunefully, a song which Fern recognised as one of Fiona's repertoire.

Gathering up her belongings, Fern shook her head. She had not imagined the coolness of Paul's greeting. 'No—really, I must go. I do have an awful lot of work to get through, I'll call you, Fiona.' With brief but firm farewells all round, she left. She began to regret it before she drove through the Camerons' gateway. She couldn't run away from all relationships for ever.

Back home her answering service was flashing. She listened to the message as she made a sandwich and instant coffee. It sounded like the prospect of another job when she called the number back. She took directions and promised to be there that afternoon. She had been more truthful than she realised when she excused herself on the grounds of work to do. She also had an article to write up for one of the glossy monthly magazines, she would do that later in the day.

By the time she had visited her new clients—this turned out to be a relatively simple kitchen reconstruction—and written the first draft of her magazine piece, Fern was bushed. She was also ready to question whether a life that consisted of little else but hard work and scratch meals was really what she had come here to find.

Maybe it had been a mistake coming. If her career was the all important thing, then the answer was a definite 'yes'. If getting her act together and making a new life for herself was what she truly wanted then, 'no'. When the cat appeared on the windowsill demanding admittance and supper she was actually pleased and knew that she had no wish to exchange her cottage, her garden or even this demanding old moggy, for city life.

She went to bed tired, but happier in herself than she had been for a long time. It was all the more shocking therefore to wake in the early hours, drenched with sweat, heart pounding and the sound of her own screams still ringing in her ears.

She got up and made herself a cup of strong sweet tea, which she carried back to bed and drank, slowly and thoughtfully, propped up against the pillows.

For the first time since she had begun to have this recurring dream, she forced herself to face the content and ask herself what it really meant. The other characters in the dream disturbed her. Was the dead man, who so resembled Paul, her lover? The man calling to her so harshly appeared to be Nigel, odd, for hitherto in her nightmares it had been Nigel's body she was forced to look at and identify, just as she had in real life. It was the powerful emotion, the fear, amounting to terror, that caused her to wake screaming.

She dropped to sleep eventually on the self-promise that she would sort out her night time terrors. Face them head on and deal with them. A good decision but it involved, she knew, seeking expert help from someone like Alex, and when morning finally came she asked herself if she was really prepared to do that?

She slept late. It was the persistent ringing of the phone that finally roused her.

'Hi!' Fiona, bursting with vitality and enthusiasm, made Fern feel old and jaded. She managed a somewhat less enthusiastic, 'Hi,' in return, reminding herself that Fiona was a valuable client.

'Can I come round and see you, there are a few things I want to ask you about the lounge room décor?'

'Sure, fine, come and have coffee with me,' Fern invited.

As she scrambled to shower and dress before she arrived, Fern thought how much she liked Fiona. Her ebullient personality was a tonic, it was also quite a new experience for her to be with someone who invariably seemed to see the bright side of any situation. She had momentarily forgotten about Beau and once more felt a sharp stab as he bounced out of Fiona's car. He was so like Bubbles. Fiona, quick to sense her distress, offered to leave him in the car.

'If you are worried about the cat?' she added. 'No need to be, Beau likes cats and I can promise he won't hurt it.'

'No, it's not that at all.' Fern hadn't given a thought to the cat. 'It's . . .' she trailed off, unable to explain without sounding as if she didn't like the little dog when, in truth, she thought him delightful.

'He won't hurt you either,' Fiona assured her with a grin. 'And he won't leave hairs, poodles don't you know.'

Fern nodded. 'I know, bring him in, don't leave him in the car, it will get too hot.'

Beau looked from one to the other of them then gave Fern a small and ingratiating wag of his pom-pom tail. In spite of herself, she smiled.

'Shut me up if I'm out of turn,' Fiona said as Fern handed her a steaming mug of coffee and indicated milk, sugar and a small plate of biscuits, 'but what is it about Beau that turns you off, most people think he's cute, or is it that you just don't like dogs?' When Fern didn't answer immediately she prompted, 'Is that it?'

Slowly she shook her head, 'No, I love dogs.'

'But you don't like poodles, lots of people don't, for some reason they don't consider them "real" dogs.'

'That's nonsense, of course they are real dogs.'

'Then for some reason you just don't like Beau,' Fiona persisted. She sounded hurt and Beau, gazing anxiously up at his mistress, sensing her unhappiness and guessing that it was in some way connected with him as his name kept popping up in the conversation, contrived to look quite tragic.

Fern, glancing down at the little dog, managed a wobbly smile at his woe-begone expression. 'I love Beau,' she said and hastily looked away from him.

'Then—I don't understand,' Fiona shrugged.

'I had a poodle, exactly like him. Her name was Bubbles. I—lost her.'

'Oh, Fern, I'm so sorry.' Fiona reached out and laid her hand on her arm in a gesture of sympathy. 'What happened? Or maybe you would rather not talk about it?'

'She was—killed, deliberately.'

For a moment she was tempted to tell Fiona everything, but her natural reticence held her back from blurting out the whole sad story to someone she really only knew on a business footing. So, all she said by way of explanation was, 'The only thing I don't like about Beau is that he reminds me of her.' She picked up the coffeepot. 'More coffee?' she asked in a tone of voice that made it clear that, for the moment at any rate, she was saying no more.

Fiona had to be satisfied with that, although she was quite sure that, as well as assuaging her curiosity, Fern would be better talking than bottling things up. Fiona watched her face close up, giving it a shuttered look, her eyes seemed to be gazing into a bleak past for a moment, then with a sigh, or a shudder, Fiona could not be sure, she was back in the moment.

'Yes—well . . .' Fern's voice was flat as she spread out her plans and colour charts. 'Tell me what your ideas are for the lounge room.'

Fiona dropped a hand and touched Beau on his soft curly head. Feeling the tension he had moved against his mistress's leg. In the face of

Fern's obvious pain, she was comforted by the contact as much as Beau.

Fern, anxious to make it clear no more sympathy was required, began to discuss her ideas for the other rooms in the house. Fiona, imagining her own feelings if anything dreadful happened to Beau, brought her attention to what Fern was saying and soon they were both totally engrossed in colours, styles, patterns, and room design.

Fern, anxious to impress Fiona with her professional ability, would have been astonished had she known that at that moment it was her friendship Fiona really craved. Her own career allowed little time for close friendships. She was more than delighted with the work Fern had already done and loved her ideas for the rest of the house. She left the cottage wondering what she could do to help her new friend to come to terms with whatever events had touched her life.

*   *   *

'I think there is a dark tragedy in Fern's life,' Fiona remarked to Alex over lunch.

'Oh, why?' Alex, his mind on the book he was struggling to write, and used to what he thought of as Fiona's 'wild imagination' at work, sounded pre-occupied.

'She has always been so odd about Beau. I asked her today if it was dogs in general, or poodles, poodles in general or Beau.'

'You mean you forced her into either saying she thoroughly disliked all poodles and him in particular or that she doted on him.'

'Oh, stop being clever and facetious and listen to me, Alex.'

'Go on then.' He sighed with resignation.

'She told me she once had a poodle exactly like him, except that it was a female.'

'I should have thought that was quite some difference,' Alex murmured.

Fiona ignored him. 'She said it was murdered.'

'Rather a strong word to describe the death of a dog, wouldn't you say?'

'Actually . . .' Fiona admitted, 'she said "killed deliberately". She seemed pretty upset about it, just like I would if someone hurt Beau. I got the impression that there was more, something she was bottling up inside her that would be better talked about.'

'And you think that I, because I am a psychologist, should be talking to her, is that what you are getting at?' He spoke lightly, but Fiona knew, by the keenness of his swift glance at her, that she had caught his attention.

Fiona nodded. 'Uh-huh,' she admitted, 'I know you like her.'

'Like as in "like", nothing else. I find her . . . interesting,' Alex conceded. 'But she will have to come to me voluntarily.'

'I am sure you won't find that hard to

139

arrange,' Fiona murmured as she reached over and pulled an orange out of the big bowl of fruit in the centre of the table. She studied it with care before beginning to peel it.

'Do you think it could be some sort of a hangover, something lingering from another life.' She spoke softly, as if to herself. 'I wonder if she dreams.' She knew the book Alex was so absorbed in writing was on the connection between dreaming and past-life memory. She also knew that he was experiencing problems finding people willing to co-operate with him and share their own experiences.

'Did she say anything about dreaming?' Alex asked sharply, giving Fiona the satisfaction of seeing she had caught his interest.

'No,' Fiona admitted, 'I just wondered, going through a traumatic experience can leave one with a residue of dreams.' She shrugged and concentrated on quartering her orange. 'Should I ask her to dinner?' she added ingenuously.

'That seems like a bright idea, little sister, and while you are about it, ask Paul too. It will be more sociable to have a foursome.' It would also, Alex knew, be easier to talk on a one to one basis with Fern if Paul was kept occupied by Fiona.

Fern's first reaction when Paul called and offered her a lift to the Camerons, a couple of nights later was to refuse and tell him she was quite capable of getting there under her own steam. But that, she quickly realised, would merely be 'cutting off her nose to spite her face'.

She had taken pains with her appearance, purely, she told herself, to maintain the semblance of a successful professional woman. A façade that held up well until Alex brought the subjects of past life recall and dreaming into the conversation over coffee.

Fern glanced swiftly across at Paul, suspecting he had told Alex of her dreams but he was deep in conversation with Fiona.

'How is your book going, Fern?' Alex was asking now.

'I'm afraid it is not,' she told him. 'But I'm not actually writing a book from scratch, I'm collecting pieces I have already written. How about you, is your book coming along well?'

'So, so,' he shrugged. 'I wonder sometimes if there is enough interest in the subject among the general public to make it viable. Do you believe in reincarnation?'

Fern shook her head. 'I haven't really thought about it.' That would have been true, she thought, before she'd met Paul. 'And I'm not sure I want to. It's a daunting prospect, coming back again and again to face the same problems. No—I don't believe in it.'

'We might face the same people, as well as the same difficulties,' Paul interjected.

Fern turned quickly towards him. She felt the remark was directed at her. She found him looking at her and to her chagrin felt a warm flush creeping up her neck.

'Not necessarily the same ones, different ones perhaps, if you work things out,' Alex told her. 'What about you, Fiona?'

'You know what I think, so why ask? I agree with Fern, that is with my head, but some part of me bobs up now and then to remind me of something I don't consciously know from this life. I get hit with déjà vu, I feel sure I have been here before, or I have done that before, and how do you explain child prodigies like Mozart?'

'And you, Paul?'

Paul's first reaction was, like Fiona, to remind Alex that they had enjoyed many similar discussions in the past, but guessing that he was following some private agenda of his own kept quiet.

Fern held her breath, afraid he would trot out his conviction that they had met before. To her relief he merely said quietly, 'I believe we keep returning till we get it right.'

'You do?' Alex seemed both pleased and surprised. 'Well, that makes one definite "no" and one definite "yes" and one half believing. If you three are a sample of people in general, then you could say at least fifty per cent of the population believe in it, throw me in on the side of the believers and it would be more.

Fairly accurate, for if you take the world population and divide it into religions you will find that more people, as a tenet of their faith, believe in reincarnation than those who, like Christians, are not supposed to, though you might well find, if they were honest, a good many do subscribe to a belief in many lives.'

'You're not on a podium you know, Alex,' Fiona reminded him. 'So spare us the lecture.'

'Okay, okay . . .' Alex smiled good humouredly at her, then turned to Paul. 'You and I have discussed this subject so often, Paul, I know your views almost as well as my own. Do you find your ideas backed up by your experiences in life?'

Fern was wishing more and more that she hadn't stayed on, this conversation was making her feel thoroughly out of it.

'Well, yes, I suppose I do. When I first met Fern, for instance, I was certain I had met her before.' He had the grace at least, Fern thought, to throw her an apologetic glance as he told Alex this.

Fiona, noting that Fern looked thoroughly embarrassed, wished Alex would get off his hobby horse. 'That always happens,' she put in tartly, 'if you want to prove something you manage to find proof all round you.' But her well-meant comment misfired, for Paul seemed to find it necessary to justify his remark.

'I was so sure that I knew her that, to our

mutual embarrassment, I greeted her as if I did. Yet it doesn't seem possible that we could ever have met before she came into my office. We have seldom been in the same state at the same time, sometimes not in the same country.' When it dawned on him that he was doing nothing to reduce her discomfiture, he turned to Fern with an apologetic half-smile.

Fern caught his eye and, for a second, it was as if they were alone. She felt the warmth creeping up her neck and her heart gave that odd flip, like a mini orgasm, as their eyes met. She returned his smile with a rather tremulous one of her own. Alex, she realised, as she brought her attention back to the others, was still pontificating. From the expression on Fiona's face, she guessed that she knew that once off on this topic, her brother took some silencing.

'I do quite a bit of hypnotherapy in my work,' he was saying now. 'In fact, you could say that is my speciality, and every now and again, clients under hypnosis appear to have gone back beyond this life. When it first happened I was fascinated, intrigued. That was when I really got interested in the whole idea of reincarnation, living more lives than one, and then I wondered if maybe we sometimes link into our other lives in the dream state, so I started taking special note of people's dreams with a reference to that.'

Fern squirmed in her seat, dreams were bad

enough at night, to be reminded of them during the daytime on a social outing was too much.

'Do you dream much?' Alex asked Paul, the one firm believer in his small audience.

Paul shook his head. 'No, or if I do, I block them out and don't remember, but Fern . . .' He stopped short, biting off his words as he realised that what he had been about to say would be the betrayal of a confidence.

Fern glared at him. 'I have the odd nightmare,' she said in a carefully controlled, level voice. 'I guess most people do—from time to time. Probably something I eat that disagrees with me.'

Paul looked as if he wanted to say more but didn't. Alex turned his attention to Fern noting that despite her casual dismissal of his theories, she looked tense, her fingers closed tightly into fists and her bottom lip caught by her teeth. She would, he thought, be an interesting subject.

'You've held the floor long enough, Alex,' Fiona complained. 'Isn't anyone going to ask me about my trip?' Seeing Fern so uptight had made Fiona feel somewhat guilty for suggesting to her brother that she might be a good source of material for his book.

'Sure, did you have a chance to see much of the country, or was it all travelling and work?' Fern responded gratefully. A few moments ago she had been wishing for her own transport so she would be free to leave whenever she wished. Now, when Paul interrupted Fiona's entertaining flow of reminiscences with a yawn, she wanted to stay on.

'Sorry!' he quickly apologised to Fiona. 'That was plain old exhaustion, not boredom, it's been one hectic day.' He turned to Fern. 'If you don't mind . . . ?'

'I've had a busy day myself,' Fern admitted. 'And I suppose you are still recovering from your tour? I hope you'll tell me more about it . . .' She trailed off, not sure when she would next see Fiona.

'Surely you are not going so early—the night is young still,' Alex demurred. He had hoped to be able to get Fern on her own. Fiona, he could see, was not very pleased to be losing Paul so early in the evening. Like him, she had probably hoped for more.

She smiled warmly at Fern. 'Thanks for coming, I'm really dying to see what you do with the rest of the house.' Turning to Paul, she remonstrated, 'Next time I see you just don't be too tired to listen to my travelogue!' Then she kissed him directly on the lips. Fern turned away; she didn't want to see his response.

Paul was the first to break the silence as he turned the car out of the drive gate. 'I'm sorry, I shouldn't have mentioned your dreams.' He spoke shortly and Fern did not think he sounded particularly contrite.

She shrugged, affecting nonchalance. 'Not to worry.' After a few moments silence she gave voice to another thought. 'I hope Alex is not planning to raid my subconscious as research for his book.'

Paul, glancing sideways in her direction, noted the light look on her face. 'You are very protective of your subconscious,' he remarked, giving way to a childish desire to needle.

This made Fern suddenly see red. 'I need to be,' she snapped, 'with all and sundry talking about it.'

'I am not "all and sundry" and I have already apologised for my thoughtless remark.' They completed the short journey in silence.

Paul wondered if he would be forgiven if he stayed the night. He no longer felt tired and Fern's averted features and stiff back made him want to shake her. Along with his anger, he could feel desire, sharp and insistent, singing in his veins. He wanted to stay the night and make love to her, but he wasn't prepared to do any more apologising, neither did he want to risk a full-scale row.

But when they reached her gate, Fern bade him a cool 'Goodnight', stepped out of the car and slammed the door, just a little too hard, behind her before walking away from him without a backward glance to disappear through her front door, which again closed with decided firmness.

Paul shot away from the kerb with rather less than his usual finesse. Women, he thought, why did they always have to get so emotional? It didn't occur to him that in this instance he, rather than Fern, was the emotional one.

Tossing as sleep eluded her, Fern refused to admit that she would have given a lot to have had Paul with her. She liked him, really liked him, yet she had choked him off almost to the point of quarrelling. She wondered how long it would take her to grasp the fact that all men were not like Nigel. She reminded herself that she had come to this quiet little town to start a new life—on her own—so could hardly complain if that was precisely what she found herself doing.

She hadn't bargained on meeting anyone as attractive as Paul, certainly not someone convinced they remembered her from a previous life. It was too bizarre. All that nonsense that had been talked tonight about past lives and reincarnation. Alex was either off his trolley or onto a good thing, using his knowledge of psychology to write a book that would appeal to the gullible masses. Well, she for one had no intention of being a guinea pig for his research.

Resolutely, she picked up her book from the bedside table, but neither the novel nor her self-administered pep-talk could still the crazy longing that engulfed her. Physical weariness finally won. She hoped, as she drifted into sleep, that if she dreamed of Paul, he would at least be alive.

If she dreamed, she had no recollection of it. She woke refreshed and ready to face whatever the new day brought and convinced that Alex and Paul had both been talking nonsense. She hummed as she made coffee and toast and fed the cat. It was still 'the' cat, not 'her' cat and she hadn't given it a name. Maybe she should, as a pledge to the future.

She put in a full morning's work, finishing, and e-mailing to the features editor, her magazine piece. With that out of the way, she concentrated on translating the ideas they had tossed around the previous evening into firm plans. Unsure of the best places to shop, she called Fiona.

'Would you like to "okay" the paperwork before I actually buy the fabrics and wallpaper?' she asked, adding, 'Perhaps you could suggest the best places to go, this is strange territory to me. I don't know the stores like I do in the city, I got most of the fabrics and things for my own place in Melbourne.'

Fiona laughed. 'You are asking the blind to lead the blind, worse, I wouldn't even know where to go in Melbourne, let alone up here.'

Fern made a quick decision, this was an important assignment, she couldn't afford to give it anything but her best shot. 'I'll go up tomorrow, if I could just bring these final plans over for you to check first.'

'I have a far better idea—why don't we go together?'

'Oh, but—are you sure?' If Fiona was with her, a choice of materials could be made there and then.

'Positive! If we choose the materials together you won't have to get my approval before work actually starts,' Fiona verbalised her own thoughts. 'It will be fun, we will have a day out. I'll pick you up at seven thirty in the morning, I enjoy driving. It'll be great, I'm looking forward to it already.'

'So am I,' Fern agreed, and meant it.

As they headed down the motorway in the freshness of early morning, Fern realised that it was a long time since she had throbbed with anticipatory excitement, as she was now. She was enjoying her new lifestyle but, as Fiona had said, a day in the city would be fun.

They found the exact fabric they were hunting for almost immediately. Fiona was impressed by Fern's knowledge of the best stores to visit.

'It's easier where you know and are known,' Fern acknowledged. 'It made it easier that we were in total agreement too!' Had they not been, they could have spent most of the day going from place to place to get just what satisfied them both. As it was, they were left free to go pleasure shopping and have a leisurely lunch before heading back with a laden car.

They were nearly home when Fiona introduced the first jarring note of the day.

'Have you reconsidered helping Alex out with his book?'

Fern was taken aback, wondering again what 'all and sundry' had been discussing behind her back. 'What do you mean "reconsider helping him"?'

Hearing the sharp note in her voice, Fiona smiled apologetically. 'Sorry, wrong word, I should have said consider, not reconsider. Alex has the idea that if you would talk about your dream experiences with him it might help him. He seems to have hit a writer's block or something at the moment. I'm sure the book would be a huge success if only he could get it finished.' She sighed and half-turned to Fern with a smile.

Fern liked Fiona, it had been a great day. She felt she owed her for she had not only commissioned her to do up her own house but suggested her to friends. But her dreams were something she did not want to discuss with anyone. She remembered Paul's somewhat derisive comment, that she was 'protective of her subconscious', and surprised herself by asking gruffly,

'Just what would "helping" Alex involve?'

Fiona shrugged. 'Oh, nothing much, just tell him about your dreams, that's all. I didn't think you would mind.'

'My dreams are usually the sort I don't want

to remember, let alone talk about,' Fern protested.

'Sometimes the best way to forget is to talk. But if you don't feel up to it . . .' She left the words hanging in the air and Fern, needled by the suggestion that she was being wimpish, found herself agreeing.

'All right,' she sighed. 'I'll talk to him, just once.' She intended to make it clear to Alex that she was just being friendly; she was not placing herself in his hands as a patient, client or whatever he liked to call the people who were prepared to lay bare their souls to him.

Fiona must have relayed the information to Alex as soon as she got home, for Fern barely had time to kick off her town shoes, dump her shopping and make herself a cup of tea before the phone rang.

'No,' she told him firmly, 'not today, Alex. I have been in Melbourne all day, I am tired, I have things to do. Tomorrow if you like, but not today.' His eagerness made her feel she had been bulldozed into the whole thing, and illogically the person she was most annoyed with was Paul. If he had kept his mouth shut about her dreaming she could have sat quietly throughout the whole conversation and Alex would not have seen her as potential material for his damn book. Somewhat grudgingly, she finally agreed to let him interview her, question her, whatever he wanted so long as he didn't intend to hypnotise her, the following day.

She had barely replaced the receiver before it rang again. This time it was Paul.

'Look,' he said without preamble, 'I really am sorry if I did anything to upset you when we were at the Camerons'. Can I offer you a peace offering, dinner tonight?'

"Well . . .' Fern was no less tired than she had been a few minutes back when she'd refused to see Alex, but taken by surprise, she was far less adamant in saying so. 'I've only just got back from Melbourne,' she hedged. 'I planned an early night.' She did not feel in the least like dressing up again and going out. But Paul had a compromise to offer.

'How about I get a takeaway and a bottle of wine and bring it round?' Fern was tempted. 'Any particular preference, Chinese, pizza, you name it, I'll get it.'

'Pizza would be great.' One didn't need to dress up or lay a splendid table to eat it, in fact fingers and a comfortable chair were perfect.

'Hmm.' Fern sighed contentedly as she licked her fingers and raised her glass, squinting at him through the warm colour of a good Australian red. 'I really enjoyed that, thanks Paul.'

'I'm forgiven then?'

'Not entirely,' she teased. 'I'll let you know after Alex has had me stretched out on his couch, or whatever, probing the secrets of my dream life.' Relaxed and full of good food and wine, she was able to sound light and self-mocking and hide the fact that she was actually feeling quite uptight about the whole thing.

Paul frowned slightly, he was not fooled by her attempt to make light of it and was truly sorry that his tongue had let her in for this. He hoped Alex would not probe too deeply and turn it into something more traumatic than helpful for her. 'Would you like me to come round and give you moral support?'

'I'll be okay,' she told him, with more confidence than she felt. 'I'm only going to do this once,' she added.

Paul looked doubtful. Would Alex be willing to stop after one session? 'Well, if you change your mind . . .' he let the words trail off before adding in a more positive tone, 'Perhaps you will find it does help, talking with a professional, I mean.'

Fern shrugged, still relaxed and mellowed by the wine. 'Maybe, I hope so.' She got up to make coffee, saying to him over her shoulder, 'But I doubt it. To be frank, I haven't found psychologists so much help in the past. I think when it gets down to the nitty gritty, the only person who can help you is yourself.' With her attention on the coffee she missed the bleak expression on his face. She hadn't really expected an answer, even so was a little surprised when he changed the subject after a brief pause as she carried the coffee over and put it down on the low table between them.

'I believe that young couple asked you to cast your professional eye over that dreadful place they have bought.'

'Yes, thanks to your recommendation, and it is not a dreadful place at all, it's a good example of the art deco period, it's the so-called improvements that have ruined it.'

Paul shrugged, that expressive rather Gallic gesture that she had noticed when they first met and had always thought odd in an Australian, or New Zealander. 'No doubt you will be able to earn a few dollars telling them how to improve on the improvements, or dispense with them altogether.'

'No doubt,' Fern agreed, matching his dry tone with a coolness of her own. She passed him his coffee and wondered what had happened to the warm relaxed feeling between them. She was not aware of having done or said anything to change it, but Paul seemed to have gone from her to some dark place of his own. She had experienced ten years ricocheting from dizzy heights to black unfathomable depths with Nigel. Now all she wanted was to live on an even keel. She got up abruptly and carried her coffee cup over to the sink.

'If you don't mind, Paul, I really am tired. It's been a busy day.' She yawned rather theatrically to press her point home. If he was going to brood, then he could do it elsewhere.

She heard Paul getting up and sensed he

was moving towards her, she still had her back to him as she fiddled at the sink rinsing out her coffee mug. 'Damn!' she had hit the tap with the mug as she reached for the draining rack and knocked the handle off. Feeling absurdly close to tears she rounded on Paul. 'Now look what you have made me do!'

'You are right. You certainly are tired and overwrought, or overtired and wrought.'

Fern knew he was tying to smooth the moment with levity. Normally it would have worked. Tonight his tone of voice and the knowledge that she was being quite unfair just incensed her further. 'I told you I was tired,' she mumbled sounding like a sulky teenager. 'I'm sorry,' she managed grudgingly.

She felt Paul come up behind her but did not turn to see the deep pools of anguish in his eyes.

'Fern . . .'

'Goodnight, Paul,' she said firmly.

With a shrug he turned on his heel and walked out, not quite slamming the door behind him.

Fern threw the broken mug in the garbage bin and wished she could dispose of her own sour mood as easily. She felt badly about the way she had sent him off. There were nicer ways to tell someone you didn't want sex just then. Suddenly, and quite perversely, she wished he had stayed, if only so that she would have known what he had been about to say when she cut him off so sharply.

CHAPTER SEVEN

Fern felt she had behaved like a spoilt and stupid schoolgirl as she tossed and turned, in spite of her claim to be tired. She felt ashamed and reflected ruefully that Paul had been right when he said she was overtired, or was it overwrought? At the moment she felt decidedly under wrought, if there was such a thing. Where was the image of herself she had been so careful to create since she had come to live here and start a new life? How on earth had she come to agree so weakly to a session with Alex? Unable to answer her own questions, she finally fell asleep. Her last thought was a promise to herself to call him first thing in the morning and wriggle out of it, if possible. She was spared her usual nightmare, but there was no escaping Paul. This time it was a crazy dream in which she was chasing him along a railway line, he was on foot and she was in a train, yet he not only gained on her but disappeared into the distance.

She woke still intending to cancel the coming meeting with Alex, but before she could do anything about it, he rang her. He seemed so genuinely pleased and grateful and she found herself saying, 'Oh, I don't know, here?' when he asked whether she wanted to go there or preferred him to come to her.

She was a bit disconcerted when he arrived to see that he had brought with him a taperecorder as well as what appeared to be a copious pile of notebooks and biros.

'I always carry spares.' He smiled when he noticed her eyes on them as he placed them on the coffee table and looked round for a power point for his taperecorder.

Fern pointed out the nearest one. 'Coffee?' she suggested, hoping to delay the whole ridiculous business.

'Afterwards, I want you relaxed not stimulated.' He smiled reassuringly. 'Don't look so worried, you won't tell me anything you don't want to, even under hypnosis.'

'But you are not going to hypnotise me, I only agreed to talk to you.'

'Then we will talk.' Alex sounded so soothing that Fern wondered if she had over reacted as she settled herself in the recliner armchair he indicated. He had carefully arranged two chairs directly opposite each other.

'Hypnotism is an emotive word,' he went on in that same soft voice. 'I just want you to sit there and relax, take a deep breath and then breath out slowly, feel yourself relaxing into the chair. We are just going to talk, nothing more, so relax, breathe deeply, let those tight muscles in your shoulders go, no need to grip the arms of the chair like that, open your fingers, let your hands just lie there on the arms, breathe deeply and re-l-a-x.'

Fern took another deep breath and, obeying that smooth voice with its repetitive suggestions, loosened her fingers and felt her shoulders sag, her eyelids grow heavy. God she was tired. When her eyes closed she sighed, powerless to stop them, and still through it, there was that soft voice urging her to let go, to relax . . .

Alex's voice seemed to be coming from both far away and close at hand, altogether a most strange sensation. 'Tell me about your dreams,' he was saying softly, insistently. She didn't want to answer, but he repeated, 'Tell me about your dreams,' and when she still didn't answer, 'You do dream, don't you, Fern?'

She nodded, her head felt heavy, her thoughts muzzy and though she thought she was speaking quite loudly and clearly she could hear her voice coming out as a soft murmur, 'Yes, I dream.'

'Good dreams?' Alex's voice, insistent, probing.

She shook her head, 'Bad dreams,' she told him. He was going to ask about them, she didn't want to tell him, didn't want to think about them, and certainly didn't want to re-live in the daytime those night-time terrors. With a supreme effort, she pulled herself up from out of the deep pit of sleep she had almost fallen into, some part of her brain reminding her that Alex himself had said, 'No-one can hypnotise you, if you don't want to be hypnotised.' She clung to that and with an effort, opened her eyes.

She looked at Alex, his hand held a biro and was poised over his note pad. She glanced at the taperecorder, it did not appear to be running. 'I'm sorry,' she told him, 'I really don't think I can talk about my dreams at the moment, not just yet.'

He shrugged, she could see from the gesture and the pulling together of his lips that he was annoyed, however, he managed a slight smile, and said lightly, 'Then we will talk about something else.'

'And I definitely did not want to be hypnotised.'

'No-one can be hypnotised against their will,' Alex repeated.

The irritation in his voice angered Fern, she was the one with the right to be annoyed. 'You can have a damn good try, though, can't you?' she rapped. The sensation that she was losing control had been frightening.

Alex sighed, put down the note pad and biro and leaned back in his chair. He appeared to be considering her, in actual fact reining in his own annoyance. He knew he had rushed things. If he was not careful he would scare her off altogether.

'Is coffee permitted now?' Fern's voice was icy, but she was no more anxious to quarrel than he was. Her sense of unreality slowly faded as she busied herself with the drink. By the time she sat down again opposite him, both of them with coffee in hand, she no longer felt so much like an interesting specimen skewered on a pin.

'What made you come to this sleepy little town, Fern?' he asked as they sipped their coffee.

'I could ask you the same thing,' she countered.

'You could, and I'll happily tell you,' Alex replied. 'Fiona and I came for that very quality, the relaxed sleepiness of the place. We needed a refuge for the times when the pressures of our respective careers and the hectic pace of city living got too much for us. We come here to charge our batteries, not to escape completely.'

'Maybe the same applies to me,' she retorted. The suggestion, however obliquely made, that she had come here to escape, to run away from something, annoyed her, maybe because of the very truthfulness of it.

'There's a difference,' he insisted. 'We still have our Melbourne home to go back to when we feel ready, but you have given away city life to bury yourself here, where no-one knows you. Why, Fern?'

'I needed a change, I had had enough of the stress of city living. Like you, I do some writing, I can do that just as well here as in Melbourne, and, thanks to Paul, and of course you and Fiona, I am getting enough work to keep the wolf from the door.'

'A bit drastic wouldn't you say, cutting yourself right off from your professional contacts and moving here? I believe you are a very successful consultant in the interior design field. I know you are in fact, I had heard of you in Melbourne, so had Fiona, we couldn't believe our good luck when Paul brought you to meet us. You've proved to be as good as your reputation. But I still can't help but wonder—why here?'

'I've told you, I needed a change and I want to write a book. I'm using the pieces I have written over the years that have appeared in various magazines. Going over them, in most cases rewriting somewhat, and making them chapters for a book.' She didn't add that at least that was what she had intended to do, as far as actually doing it, well, she hadn't got far yet.

Alex seemed to be waiting for her to continue. Fern found herself speaking to fill the silence. 'Things had been a bit, well, traumatic.' What a masterly understatement. 'I felt I needed a fresh start.'

Alex looked at her thoughtfully, making Fern feel like an interviewee for a job. He startled her by asking, 'Will you write about the work you have done for us?'

'Well, yes, probably. I have good photos of your kitchen before and after, and I am rather proud of it, it is such a complete transformation.'

'I see.' Alex's voice was cool.

Looking at him, Fern felt a frisson of dislike. Hitherto, his startling good looks had left her unmoved, she had been able to appraise his appearance with no stirring of emotion, either way.

'Don't you think . . .' he went on, 'it would only be fair if you—co-operated—with me and told me something about your dream life in exchange for our kitchen?' The smile with which he said the words did not touch his eyes.

'A deal?' Fern's cool tones did not betray her annoyance. 'Certainly, but not today, if you don't mind, Alex.' She turned her back on him and began clearing and tidying coffee things, making rather more fuss than the simple task warranted.

Taking the hint, Alex got up, unplugged his unused taperecorder, and gathered up his belongings.

'We'll call it a day—for the moment.' As he looked up, the frown dissolved in a brilliant smile and for a moment Fern was charmed. 'My place I think, next time. Thanks for the coffee.' With a farewell nod he turned and walked out, leaving Fern to gape after him.

163

As she listened to his car moving away, her anger, free to boil over without Alex as a witness, made the need for action imperative. It wasn't just Alex she was mad with, it spilled over to herself for letting herself in for what she felt had been a humiliating experience, and to Paul who had, however innocently, let her in for this. She snatched up her car keys, apologised to the cat for failing to produce the meal he seemed to be expecting, and hurtled out of the house. Only when she was halfway to Paul's office did it occur to her that it might have been more prudent to call him first.

'When will he be back?' Fern cut short Dot's apologies for Paul's absence. The woman irritated her with her arch smiles and innuendoes about the relationship between herself and Paul. He had laughed when he told her that she had referred to Fern as 'your girlfriend' with the comment that 'poor old Dot is a sucker for romance.' Fern had not been amused at the time, nor was she now.

'He shouldn't be long.' Dot looked at her watch then up at the clock on the wall. 'Does he know you are here, or shall I let him know?'

'I'm not here on business.' She watched Dot's eyebrows arch to form question marks and could have bitten her tongue. 'I'll wait.' By the time she had spent ten minutes desultorily flicking through a pile of rather tired looking magazines in the hope of finding something of interest, her annoyance had shifted focus slightly. It was Paul's tardy arrival rather than his big mouth that was the focus of her anger now. Never one to harbour anger for long, she was debating whether to stay and confront him, or whether to leave with her pride intact, when she saw him through the glass panel of the door and jumped to her feet.

'Fern!' She could not miss the way his face lit up when he saw her, while it warmed her at the same time it annoyed her for she knew that busybody at the reception desk had noticed it too. 'How lovely to see you. Cup of coffee?'

'No thanks.' She shook her head, having coffee with Paul would be very agreeable, but it would undermine what she had come to say.

'Is something wrong, can I help you?'

'Nothing really, Paul. I just came here on impulse. I'm sorry, I'm sure you are busy.' She turned towards the door, blushing and stammering, wishing she had never come. All she had achieved was embarrassment in front of both Paul and the drongo at reception.

Paul glanced at his watch. 'Come and have lunch?'

'I don't think . . .' Fern began, but he cut her refusal short.

'Yes, it'll have to be a fairly quick snack as I have another appointment in three quarters of an hour. A salad roll and a coffee at the milk bar?' He smiled. 'Please!'

She shrugged. 'Okay, just a snack.'

They ordered their rolls and coffee and

settled in a corner table.

'Now,' Paul demanded, 'what is the problem?'

Fern shrugged. 'No problem.' By now her morning encounter with Alex was receding and she was remembering that he was Paul's friend.

'If you say so.' It was Paul's turn to shrug dismissively now. 'All the same you looked pretty het up.'

Fern bridled. 'I was not "het up" as you put it, just slightly annoyed.'

'And was your slight annoyance anything to do with me?' Paul asked in the careful reasonable voice that one assumes to deal with a difficult child. Fern found it irritating and answered more sharply than she intended.

'You've got it in one,' she snapped. 'I've spent the morning with Alex, thanks to you.'

'Was that so bad?' he asked mildly. 'And why blame me?'

Fern ignored the first question. 'Because you mentioned my dreams to him which gave him the idea of interviewing me, for his book.'

'So . . .?' He raised quizzical eyebrows above his salad roll.

'He hypnotised me. No . . .' She held up one hand in an imperious gesture to silence him, 'don't tell me no-one can be hypnotised against their will, that is what he said, all the same . . .' she trailed off, suddenly unsure, had she really been hypnotised, or just pleasantly relaxed?

'Do you think you revealed all your dark past, is that the problem?'

'Of course not, I didn't reveal, as you so dramatically say, anything,' Fern retorted.

'How do you know, if you were under hypnosis?' Paul asked reasonably. Glaring at him across the small table Fern saw he was amused. He could be exasperating.

'That's not the point.'

'Which is?'

'That you, telling Alex about my dreams, sparked his interest and now I've let myself in for another session. He suggested a sort of deal, I let him probe my dreams as research for his book and in return I can use before and after photos and write up their kitchen for my book.'

'Fair enough. But what about the hypnosis, why does the idea bother you so?'

'Oh you're being so logical,' Fern complained.

Paul bit off the retort that she was being illogical. Having persuaded her to lunch with him he did not want to waste the time quarrelling. He reached across the small table and touched her hand gently and repeated his question, adding, 'Hypnosis isn't painful, Alex is an expert, you would be safe in his hands.'

His voice was soft, he sounded as if he really cared, Fern thought. She met his eyes and the tenderness and concern in them made her

167

heart lurch and her fears seemed groundless. 'I guess I'm just being silly,' she murmured. 'I suppose it is the idea of losing control, perhaps telling him things I would rather keep to myself.'

*   *   *

Alex ushered her into the small room he used as a study. Fern had seen it briefly when Fiona was giving her the grand tour of the house. She looked round her now with interest, a Holland blind was down more than half-way. When Alex moved across to it, she thought he intended to raise it, but instead, he pulled it down to the bottom of the window, further dimming the light. Fern was about to protest, but he forestalled her.

'The sun shines on my laptop screen, makes it difficult to see.' It sounded reasonable enough and Fern felt it would be ungracious not to accept this explanation. He pointed to an armchair. 'Make yourself comfortable, please.' Somewhat reluctantly Fern sat down. 'It is a recliner,' Alex told her, 'put your hand down the right side and pull that lever.'

She did as instructed, and immediately a foot rest shot up and as her feet went up, her body automatically slid further back and into the chair. It was certainly comfortable, also not too easy to leap up from, not swiftly or with dignity anyway. It was a chair created for

168

relaxation. Alex had put a disk on his CD player and the soft, ambient music washed over and through her, weaving its soothing spell. She closed her eyes and took a deep sighing breath. As she did so, the sort of perfume that matched the music wafted towards her. Incense, she thought dreamily, Alex must be burning incense. With all her senses assaulted in this pleasurable manner, Fern was more than ready to accede to his request to 'Relax—let—go—and listen to my voice.'

She didn't need to be told that her eyelids were feeling heavy, no way could she open her eyes, or that the same heavy feeling was affecting her hands resting on the arms of the chair.

Alex's voice was clear and ignoring it was not an option, even though it seemed to be coming from way off. He was asking about her childhood.

'Go back as far as you can remember—as far as you—till you are a small child—a baby . . .' He paused, then in a soft voice asked, 'Where you are now?'

'I'm . . . yes. I'm in my pram.' She sounded surprised, but it was pleasant enough. She was lying in her pram outdoors, under a tree, above her she could see the pattern of the leaves moving, tossing and dancing in the light breeze, then suddenly nothing—only blackness—and a sense of falling, falling.

'No, I'm not there any more, I seem to be falling, I must have been tipped out. I'm going down, down, down through a dark tunnel.' Her voice rose in panic, she could not stop herself. But even as she cried out, her feet seemed to hit the ground and the darkness receded. She sighed, 'That's better!'

From somewhere far away she could hear a vaguely familiar voice. She ignored it and looked round at her immediate surroundings instead. She appeared to be in a bedchamber, as old-fashioned as the word itself. The wooden floor was covered in mats, the single wooden bed with a carved headboard was covered in a bright patchwork quilt, the dressing table had a hairbrush, a comb, some odd pins and ribbons, a phial of perfume but no make-up. There was one chair, straight backed with a rush seat, a chest or tallboy on which stood a single candle and a free-standing mirror, old and spotted. She crossed the room to look at herself. How young she looked, her rich auburn hair was pulled back from her face and secured with combs just behind her ears, from there it fell in soft ringlets almost to her shoulders. Her dress was a deep emerald green which, she noticed, brought out the green in her eyes. It reached the floor and below it her feet were clad in slippers that could have been made of the same material. She felt satisfied with her appearance and knew also that she was happy with her lot. If this was a dream, she thought, then it was very pleasant. The thought reminded her that she was supposed to be answering questions about her dreams. She could hear that distant voice now asking her where she was. Before she could answer it was over-ridden by another, louder, more insistent, more familiar voice.

'Mistress Elizabeth, Mistress Elizabeth . . .' It drew closer accompanied by footsteps, then a tap on her door. 'Mistress Elizabeth . . .' the plump middle aged woman in the cap and garb of a domestic servant, sounded both puffed and exasperated. 'Did you not hear me call you— your father wishes to speak with you, he directed me to inform you that it was important.' Having delivered her message the older woman turned with a final, 'Haste ye now,' and began to descend the flight of stairs that had made her so breathless when she climbed them.

Fern once more became aware of the soft, insistent male voice questioning her about her identity. 'I am Elizabeth Carney, I am fifteen years old and I have a summons from my father who is Squire Carney. He is an impatient man, so I cannot talk any more.' *With that she set off lightly down the wooden stairs in the wake of her one time nurse, now the house-keeper at Carney Hall.*

The woman was waiting for her at the foot of the stairs, she laid a restraining hand on her arm, looked at her anxiously, then twitched her collar straight and pushed back a stray tendril of hair behind her ear. 'Go you in,' she said with a slight push in the direction of the room that was her father's special sanctum, the place where he conducted business, interviewed his tenants and upbraided Elizabeth on the rare occasions that he felt his only child needed it. When the woman touched her arm lightly and whispered, 'He has company,' she felt a tremor of anxiety. 'Tis our neighbour,' she added.

She tapped lightly on the door which was not latched and pushed it open when her father barked, 'Enter!'

He was seated behind the big table that served as his desk. There was a striking similarity between them, though his auburn hair was faded and flecked with grey, as was his beard, and his face creased and weathered by almost forty summers. His eyes softened when they fell on her, but did not meet hers. Instead he looked down at some papers on his desk. As always, she felt a surge of love for him. The relationship between them was unusual, in some ways she had been raised as a boy which had given her an independence not common in young maidens, and at almost sixteen she was still not promised in marriage. As she entered the room her father turned his gaze away from her and faced the man sitting to his left and almost in shadow, only then did Fern look away from him and directly at his visitor and knew with a dreadful clarity why she had been summoned.

172

Sir John Fitzwilliam was a widower, a contemporary of her father. His wife had died in childbed, the child itself surviving her only by a couple of days. Since then he had lived alone in his large manor house farming his land with a ruthless efficiency that had made him a wealthy man. Fern did not need to see the marriage contract to know she had been sold like a prize heifer.

'No!' she protested but the man in the chair merely smiled a slow smile of triumph. As she stared at him he swam hazily in her vision and she saw it was Nigel.

She opened her eyes to find herself staring at Alex Cameron. He too was smiling, it seemed with the same faintly triumphant look.

Fern blinked and looked around her, wondering what had woken her. She yawned and stretched, feeling at the same time refreshed and clear-headed and confused at finding herself in Alex's sanctum at the Camerons' house. Then she remembered, she was here because Alex had asked her to come and submit to his probing about her dreams.

'I hope that was helpful to you?' she endeavoured to keep the ironic note out of her voice.

'Very, thank you.' Alex patted the taperecorder standing between them. 'I have it here.'

'You mean, I—talked?' Fern was horrified.

'You did,' Alex assured her. His eyes shone

173

with a barely concealed excitement. 'Do you remember anything, Fern?'

She leaned back, closed her eyes and thought. 'Yes, yes I do. I seemed to be much younger, only in my teens, I was dressed in a green dress, rather old-fashioned.' She paused, frowning slightly as she tried to remember. 'Everything was old-fashioned—very—and somehow I think it was England, not Australia.'

Alex nodded, barely able to curb his impatience. 'Go on,' he urged, 'what happened then?'

'He said there was something very important he had to say . . . she screwed up her eyes and frowned as she tried to remember. 'But I can't remember what it was, or perhaps I didn't wait around to be told, I'm sorry.' She was silent for a moment, then with a slight smile added, 'I was quite pretty I think.'

'I'll play the tape back to you.' He pressed the re-wind button, turned up the sound, then hit 'play'.

Fern kept her eyes closed; there was something rather embarrassing about listening to her own voice recounting experiences that seemed to belong to someone else. First she talked about her earliest memory as a baby, a soft smile played round her lips as she heard herself describe the pleasure of lying in her pram under a shady tree and watching the movement of the leaves overhead and the play

174

of sunlight and shade. She felt totally at peace and utterly relaxed. Her smile was replaced with a slight frown as she listened to her own description of whooshing down a dark tunnel. There was a pause and then her voice seemed to change. Absurdly, she sounded as if she had shed a dozen years or so as she gave her slow and hesitant description of her physical appearance. She spoke more confidently when she mentioned the other people and she could hear both anger and despair in her voice when they came to the point where she realised just why her father had demanded her presence. But throughout she spoke haltingly, almost unwillingly, her answers drawn from her by his voice softly but insistently asking questions. When he flicked the 'off' switch, her eyes flew open and she stared at him.

'You see how exciting that was?'

'No,' Fern said in a flat voice. This was true, that she could actually go back and remember a time when she was a young baby was much more interesting than a rather mundane dream.

'But don't you realise what happened?' Alex demanded. 'The significance of the tunnel?'

'What significance?' Fern asked sharply. 'It was just the dividing line between my memories and the dream, probably the point at which I dropped off to sleep.'

He shook his head impatiently. No . . . well I suppose it was, in a way.' He leaned forward

175

again toward Fern, his eyes glittering. 'When you went down that tunnel . . .' he paused for dramatic effect, 'you accessed another life.'

Fern laughed out loud, 'Oh, no, Alex, that is quite absurd. For one thing, I simply do not believe in reincarnation, nor do I want to, one life is quite enough for me.' She moved to get up. 'No Alex, I'm sorry, but all you have succeeded in convincing me of is the power of clever suggestion over a relaxed mind.' Yet even as she spoke, her disturbing night dreams seared her memory. Could it be possible after all that they were nothing to do with her present life?

Fern was surprised to find that far from feeling stressed out, she actually felt refreshed and agreed to another session. Driving home, Fern debated within herself whether she would call in on Paul in his office, but decided against it. Much as she would like to talk to him and discuss her morning's experiences, she was loathe to let him think she was running after him. It was serendipity to find his car parked at her gate.

'Hi, have you come for lunch?'

'Well . . .'

'It will be pot-luck I'm afraid.' she warned him, 'and not much "pot" about it either, more like bread and cheese.'

'Suits me.' He latched the gate behind them and followed her up the garden path.

The cat rubbed round his legs as Paul

waited for Fern to open up the door. 'I hope he isn't doing that with malicious intent,' he commented, brushing a dusting of white hairs off the dark fabric.

'I think he likes you, that's all. Were you thinking of Thomasina . . . ?' She trailed off, he would not know what she was talking about. But he surprised her.

'I was, she gloated about leaving hairs on the dark suit of the man she disliked.' He bent down and stroked the cat who had managed to get into the house with them. 'Read that book too, have you, old fellow?'

'Possibly,' Fern responded dryly, 'I have a copy. I love Paul Gallico's books, fairy tales for adults.'

'Like all fairy tales, there is more to them than meets the eye.

'Oh, all that about reincarnation, that is what makes it into a fairy tale,' she insisted.

The cat was demanding the meal he obviously considered long overdue. She reached for the can opener, mentally reviewing the contents of her fridge and wishing it were as easy to feed a man as a cat. Bread and cheese was all she had. At least she had three varieties of cheese, a nice crusty loaf, and fresh tomatoes. The coffee, her first consideration, was already filling the kitchen with its wonderful aroma.

Paul drew up a stool for himself and began to cut the loaf. 'Thomasina is all about reincarnation,' he pointed out.

Fern helped herself to bread. 'Fantasy,' she said briefly, reaching for the cheese.

They ate in silence for a few moments then Paul asked, 'Your session with Alex, how did it go? Did he convert you to the idea of re . . .'

'No, Paul, he did not, and neither will you, so please—do me a favour and give the subject a rest.' She forgot that earlier, when she saw his car at the gate she had welcomed the prospect of telling Paul about her morning. 'Alex believes he took me back into another life. I don't. Under the influence of his suggestions my imagination went into overdrive, that's all. I don't believe in this reincarnation thing, and to tell you the truth I don't want to. I am finding this life more than enough to cope with and I have no desire to wander off into another one.' She tried for a lighter note, 'I might even find myself married to the same person. That . . .' she said decidedly, 'would be more than I could cope with.'

Paul did not answer immediately, he looked at her with one eyebrow raised and a slightly mocking smile curving his lips. 'Good, then you won't need warning.'

'Paul, what *are* you talking about?' Fern was exasperated. She watched Paul slowly stick the point of the cheese knife into the wedge he had just cut and waited for him to explain.

He merely shrugged slightly and ignoring

her question said, 'By the way, how is the book coming along?'

But Fern was not to be side-tracked. 'Oh, fine,' she said, casually dismissive, 'but what do you feel it necessary to warn me about?'

Paul looked directly at her then, as if weighing up her reaction to his words. 'Alex.'

'What are you talking about?' Fern repeated. 'He's your friend.'

Paul sighed, realising he had either said too much, or not enough. 'I don't want you to get hurt,' he finally muttered,

'It was your idea for me to get psycho-analysed or whatever by Alex,' Fern reminded him.

'Talk to him, get counselling, I thought he might help you with those nightmares of yours—he helped me.'

It was only afterwards that Fern remembered Paul saying Alex had helped him and wondered, briefly, why he had needed help.

Now, she was merely irritated when he added, 'I feel responsible.'

'Well you don't have to feel responsible for me . . .' she told him, carrying their dishes over to the sink, 'I quite enjoyed my session with Alex today, I found it restful and relaxing.'

Paul shrugged yet again, it had become a familiar gesture to Fern, looked at his watch and stood up. 'I'll have to get going, I have an appointment in ten minutes,' he told her, but he didn't go immediately. Instead he paused at the door, still with that slightly anxious look on his face reminding Fern of an over protective parent. She didn't want him to look at her like that and she certainly didn't appreciate what she considered his fussing. 'I'll be off,' he repeated, then as if he really couldn't help himself. 'Take care!' and the door closed behind him.

Fern tried to dismiss him from her thoughts, and with the last plate in the draining rack went to her computer. Enough of fantasy for one day, working on her book would ground her. But in spite of all her good intentions it was Paul who filled her thoughts as she waited for the laptop to warm up. She could not dismiss the strange link, almost recognition, that there was between them, his appearance in her bizarre dreams and Alex's conviction that he had taken her back in time to a former life. Was it credible that there was something in the idea of reincarnation after all?

There was something else nibbling round her thoughts, something Paul had said. Then it came back, flashing into her mind as the computer hummed to life. *'He helped me.'* That was it, but why should Paul, who struck her as having it all together, as much as, or more than, most people need help—especially from Alex?

CHAPTER EIGHT

Fern found her thoughts kept turning to her lunch with Paul. She had planned to spend the afternoon putting her book together. Most of the pieces published in various magazines were on her computer; it was simply a question of stringing them into chapters and getting permission from the various editors to re-use them. But memories of her time with Paul and, to a lesser extent, her session with Alex kept intruding, however hard she tried to keep them out. The ringing phone was a welcome distraction.

'I am not a property valuer,' she told the caller who had picked up one of her business cards in Paul's office and would like her to look at a house they were considering.

'Oh, I realise that, but I thought if you could just give me some idea of what we could do with the place and a rough idea of the cost . . .'

'Well, yes—all right,' Fern agreed somewhat reluctantly knowing that she would do no work on her own book if she went. But she had left her cards in Paul's office after all.

She found a miner's stone cottage quite similar to her own. It was in good repair but hadn't seen a paintbrush in twenty years or more. Her caller turned out to be the male half of a young couple, high on taste and enthusiasm but low on cash. When she showed them her folio with the 'before and after' photos of her own cottage they were over the moon and couldn't wait to get in touch with Paul and clinch the deal.

'Come and look at my place,' Fern invited spontaneously, 'before you make a final decision.'

'Great!' they enthused in unison. 'Now?'

'Oh . . .' Fern hadn't expected this, but a quick mental tour of her cottage assured her it was tidy. 'Why not? No time like the present is there?'

The young woman could barely contain her enthusiasm when she saw what Fern had done with the cottage. 'I just love it, don't you, darling?'

Her husband shrugged slightly and smiled at Fern with a slight lift of the eyebrows that conveyed perfectly his helplessness. She smiled back, she liked them and the cottage was the sort of job she really loved.

Fern made tea and put biscuits on the table while the couple called Paul on his mobile phone. 'We are at Fern Barclay's cottage,' she heard the wife telling him. She turned round and mouthed something which Fern guessed was asking if it would be okay if Paul came round, then turned back to the phone. 'That's great, see you in a few minutes.'

She shrugged apologetically. 'Hope you don't mind, he said he was only just round the corner, wherever that is, so he's coming straight here.'

Fern added a fourth cup and saucer to the table to show she didn't mind. Fate, it seemed, was determined to throw her like a bouncing ball into Paul's orbit.

Feeling a little de trop as the young couple signed up for the cottage, Fern went to the door to see if the cat was there, intending to give him a saucer of milk.

'Oh, you've got a cat,' the young woman exclaimed, rushing forward to make friends with him as he trotted in, yelling as usual. 'Isn't he beautiful?'

'Is he?' Fern was doubtful.

'She thinks every cat is beautiful,' the husband told her.

'But they are, and this one I would say has a bit of Siamese in him.'

'You would?' In spite of herself, Fern was becoming attached to the cat—but beautiful, and part Siamese?

'Definitely, that loud voice is a dead giveaway,' the wife explained. 'What do you call him?'

Fern did not like to admit that she never called him anything but Cat when so much admiration had been expended on him. She was about to say Thomasina, then realised he was a 'he' not a 'she'.

'Boss, because he shouts at her,' Paul supplied confidently.

Surprisingly, or maybe because it sounded a bit like 'puss', the cat stalked over to the woman's outstretched hand when she called him.

'Well, Boss, it looks like you've got a name,' Fern told him as she replenished his empty saucer with milk as the door closed on her visitors. After a second she sat down at the table and poured herself another cup of tea. She was sipping it thoughtfully when Paul tapped on the door, walking in even as he did so. Fern picked up the teapot as he sat down opposite her.

He nodded. 'Penny for them?' he said as she filled his cup. She remembered him saying that before and the responsive chord it had caught in her memory. It did the same now, and as before she reminded herself that it had been one of Gran's favourite remarks. 'You look pensive,' he told her.

'To tell you the truth I was feeling a tad guilty,' she admitted. 'I hope the Stones didn't feel that you and I had colluded to drum up dollars and business for ourselves?'

'I'm sure they didn't, and even if we had they are benefiting.' He grinned at her reassuringly.

'I suppose so,' she said doubtfully. 'It's just that they seemed so nice, so—innocent somehow.' She looked up and smiled. 'Anyway, thank you for giving the cat a name, I guess I'll stick with it.'

They sipped their tea in a companionable silence, Boss's thrumming purr making a soothing background noise and giving the moment a mantle of cosy domesticity.

'When do you have another session with Alex?' Paul broke the comfortable silence with his question.

'Never I hope,' Fern was about to retort. With the prospect of another house makeover she would have little time to take part in Alex's experiments with time.

But before she spoke Paul went on, 'I should call it a day if I were you.'

His words sparked off all Fern's contrary independence. 'Damn it all Paul, it was more or less your idea and now you say, stop. It wasn't such a bad experience, quite—interesting in fact. I wouldn't mind it again—if he asks me.'

'Oh, he'll ask you. But I thought the last thing you wanted was someone probing into your dream life.'

When she didn't answer, Paul raised one eyebrow.

'Don't look at me like that,' she snapped. 'Sure, I came here for peace and privacy, and revealing my inner self to someone I scarcely know does not come into that category, but somehow it didn't seem like that with Alex.' She considered adding that she had been a different person but that would sound like admitting to something she was far from sure about.

Confused, Paul tried to sound conciliatory.

'I thought when I first suggested that you consult Alex it might help—your dreams . . .' he trailed off in the face of Fern's scowl and shrugged helplessly.

'Well, don't think. Just because you seem to feature in most of my nightmares doesn't give you the right to get me psycho-analysed . . . just because I keep dreaming of you dead doesn't mean anything.' She stopped, aghast, as she realised that she had admitted to Paul his prominence in her dreams. She could only hope he had not heard. Unwilling to look him squarely in the face Fern picked up the cups and saucers from the table and banged them down a little too hard on the draining board. She turned the tap on full blast and began to rinse them, very noisily, hoping that Paul would get the hint and leave, or at the very least change the subject. He did neither and eventually she was forced to turn around and face him.

'How did I die?' The question asked in a quiet voice was the last thing she expected him to say. 'You said you dreamed I was dead, how did I die?' He repeated the question as she stood there, her back to the sink.

'Does it matter?' She tried to sound uninterested, casual.

'I think so, if it is causing you to have bad dreams, and before you say it is none of my business, I think it is. After all it is my death we are talking about.'

'Your death, my dreams, the argument is spurious. I dream of other people too. Nigel— my husband—for one. I have had nightmares about him ever since he—died.' She stopped abruptly, afraid of revealing more of herself than was comfortable.

Paul wanted to ask about her husband, how had he died, but Fern rushed on.

'It was his body I used to see—now it's yours.' And the moment was lost as her voice faded to a whisper.

Paul felt there was something significant in his body taking the place of her dead husband in Fern's dreams. But did he want to find out what it was? He wasn't at all sure. He finally filled the silence with the question he had nearly asked before. 'What happened to your husband, in real life I mean? And what happened to me in your dream?' She ignored the first question, merely saying laconically, 'Oh, my husband killed you in my dream.'

'A crime passionel?'

'He thought we were lovers,' she mumbled, suddenly embarrassed. 'But I think there was more to it, a political motive as well.' Fern hesitated, searching for a memory that seemed just out of reach. 'You wore such different clothes, I think my husband must have been a puritan—a roundhead . . . while you . . .' Fern smiled softly as the dream came back.

'I was a cavalier,' Paul supplied. 'I could never have been a roundhead.'

Fern looked at him then, seeing him as she had in her dreams, handsome, laughing, sumptuously dressed. Her own personal 'laughing cavalier', and she knew that her love for him and her own royalist sympathies put her in danger and were what made her so afraid.

'I knew we had met before.' Paul's voice brought her sharply back to the here and now.

'In the closing years of the sixteenth century?' Fern asked. 'You can remember so far back?'

'It seems you can,' Paul retorted.

'I can't remember, I just dreamed it, as far as I can recall from the dream, he had no real proof but only suspected us of having a liaison. I didn't actually see you killed, he had your dead body brought to the house to show me.' Involuntarily she shuddered as she remembered that scene in her dream. 'Let's change the subject, I'd really rather not talk about it,' she told him with an air of finality. It was true, she didn't want to talk about it, or think about it, she didn't want to recall the dream and, above all, she didn't want to dream it again. She turned back to the sink and, forgetting she had already done it, washed their cups again.

'Nice weather we are having,' Paul commented in a bland voice, a slight smile playing round his lips.

'Yes . . .' Fern agreed, then seeing the twinkle in his eye she threw the tea towel at him.

Paul laughed, catching it deftly. 'We won't quarrel about what happened nearly four hundred years ago,' he said as he tossed it back to her.

'We will not,' she agreed. 'That young couple you referred to me were delightful.' Determined to change the subject, 'They seem to want their cottage to look just like this,' she added.

'Imitation is the sincerest form of flattery,' he remarked cryptically.

Fern chose to ignore that. 'I took to them at once, I felt comfortable, at home with them, you know what I mean.'

'Yes—I liked them myself. How do you feel about the Camerons?'

'I really like Fiona, we get on well. I think I am a tad scared of Alex.' Frowning slightly, she tried to be fair. 'Or maybe I am afraid of what he will make me find out about myself.' Fern wondered, even as she spoke, if that were true, or was her real fear the power Alex might exert over her mind? 'Have you ever been hypnotised, Paul?'

'As a matter of fact—yes,' he answered shortly giving Fern the impression that he didn't intend to talk about it.

'You know what I mean then,' she retorted,

her voice cool.

'It helped me through a difficult period in my life,' he said enigmatically as he walked to the door. 'Thanks for the tea, I guess I'll be seeing you.'

Their relationship, Fern thought, had a tendency to move at least one step back for every two forward. What relationship? That was the last thing she had come in search of when she left Melbourne. All the same . . . with an effort she switched her mind to her ideas for the Stones' cottage. It was quite a challenge to plan it so that it was sufficiently like her own without mere duplication. She was glad to have the work as for the moment refurbishment on the Camerons' house seemed to have stalled. She had her book to work on but that would not, for some while at any rate, actually bring in an income and after the money she had spent on her own cottage, she was in danger of becoming cash strapped.

Her heart leapt when there was a tap at the door. Paul must have come back for something. 'Oh,' she tried not to sound too disappointed when she faced Fiona.

'May I come in?'

'Of course!' Fern moved aside to let her in. She pushed her rough sketches to one side on the table but not before they had caught Fiona's eye.

'Oh, may I see? Is this for our place or somewhere else?' she asked.

'Actually, those are for a cottage rather like this that a young couple have just bought,' Fern told her, suppressing a twinge of guilt that she was not actually working on the Cameron's plans.

'Mmmm—looks nice,' Fiona said approvingly as she picked up the rough sketches. 'As a matter of fact, I came to see if you have any ideas yet on the rest of our place?'

'Yes, I have . . .' Fern was thankful to be able to tell her. 'Look, these are the sketches I have done for the lounge room. I thought a lot of white, or off-white, a sort of creamy, magnolia shade to get some light in. It is rather dark at the moment, don't you think?'

'I certainly do,' Fiona agreed as she took the coloured sketch Fern was handing her from her folder. She frowned slightly. 'You don't think it is a bit too white? Apart from keeping it clean, I don't want it to look like a hospital ward.' Her smile took the criticism from her words.

Fern moved to her side and studied the sketch with her. 'We could change the off-white carpet for a light rose or pale green, and we could have toning curtains, instead of white, and plenty of bright scatter cushions on the lounge suite, I thought white leather for that and magnolia coloured walls.' With a few deft strokes of her pencil and coloured crayons Fern showed Fiona what she meant.

'Great, I really like it now. And what about Alex's consulting room or den or whatever he likes to call it, have you any great ideas for that? He seems to be getting rather impatient.' Fiona laughed. 'I am afraid we are both a bit like that, we like things done yesterday if not before, once we have made up our mind, and what about the bathroom?'

Fern thought regretfully of the book she was endeavouring to put together, that it seemed was destined for the back burner for the time being.

'Actually,' Fiona told her, 'I didn't really come to harass you, but to ask you to come to dinner tomorrow night and to deliver a message from Alex, he wants to know when you will be ready for the next session.'

'Any time,' Fern said airily. 'Actually, it wasn't as bad as I imagined it might be.'

'You sound almost as if you enjoyed it?'

'It was interesting, and I did make a bargain with him.' Fern smiled. 'And thanks for the invitation, I would like to come.'

'Great, I'll expect you about seven.' She moved to the door as she spoke, turning with her hand on the knob to add, almost as an afterthought, 'I'm asking Paul too, so I expect he will give you a lift.'

Fern closed the door behind Fiona and walked thoughtfully back into the cottage. She was glad Paul was going, of course she was, but unreasonably irritated at Fiona's assumption that he would give her a lift, as if—she thought—she were a parcel, or worse—as if they were a couple, an item. She had no wish to be a couple with anyone; her wounds were still too raw for that.

At least, she thought, she would not have to go back to the city with her tail between her legs, with the Stones' commission as well as the Camerons', she had plenty of work to keep her busy. So, she had better get down to it. She flicked the answering service on and once more sat down in front of her laptop. Barely an hour later she was interrupted by the phone. Automatically, she tuned in to the incoming message, it was Paul, simply requesting her to call him back, probably arranging to pick her up, but when she returned his call he told her that he had a prior engagement and was unable to accept the invitation.

'I didn't like to leave a blunt message like that on your machine,' he explained. Fern wished he had, she would not have had to struggle to sound bright and uncaring.

She toyed with the idea of not going herself, but she had no real excuse and felt it could offend the Camerons who were, after all, extremely good clients. She didn't analyse her disappointment that she was not, after all, going to spend an evening in Paul's company.

She didn't sound as if she cared at all, Paul thought ruefully as the line went dead. He stood for a moment staring absently at the phone still in his hand, surprised at how hurt he felt. She had seemed so different when they made love—he had begun to hope . . . Catching the drift of his own thoughts he reined them in, emotional involvement was not for him. 'Who are you fooling?' he muttered aloud to himself. There was something about Fern Barclay that got under his skin and he wanted her—desperately. He felt a sharp stab of jealousy as he thought of her with Alex Cameron.

Fern shrugged off the twinge of disquiet she felt when she noticed that Fiona's car seemed to be missing from its usual place, after all, there could be any number of reasons why it was not visible, she mused, waiting for the door to open.

'Fern . . .' the welcome in Alex's voice matched his smile, 'lovely to see you, come along in.'

As she followed him into the lounge room she cast a professional eye over it, visualising it made over according to the ideas she and Fiona had thrashed out the day before. 'Um—yes please . . .' she realised Alex was offering her a sherry from the decanter in his hand. She took the glass from him and dropped down onto the sofa, the nearest seat. Alex poured his own drink then took his place beside her. Sipping her sherry, Fern listened for some sound that would tell her Fiona was about.

There was none.

'I'm so glad you still came, even though Paul couldn't and now Fiona has taken off somewhere.' He smiled, and Fern imagined she could already feel his hypnotic power.

'Where is Fiona?' she asked, her voice sounding unnaturally high.

'Don't worry, she left us a very nice cold meal all ready,' Alex assured her. What they would eat was the least of Fern's concerns at the moment.

'When will she be back?' she tried not to sound too anxious.

Alex shrugged. 'Tonight probably. Depends, she may not make it till tomorrow morning.'

Fern gulped her drink too fast, it caught her throat and she coughed. She wondered if escape was possible, hard on the heels of that thought came another, that she was over reacting to the situation. But she still wondered what had called Fiona away after she had expressly asked her to come.

Alex looked amused, as if he knew exactly what she was thinking. 'So you and I can enjoy a pleasant working dinner.'

She smiled, 'Of course Alex,' and reached down for her briefcase with the sketches she had done, mentally telling herself to grow up and behave like the mature and sophisticated person she thought she was.

She passed the sketches to Alex, he looked at them intently then frowned as he asked,

"Well, yes, these look splendid, but what about the plans for my study?'

'I'm sorry Alex, but Fiona just asked for these yesterday—and as . . .' she tailed off uncomfortably then added hastily, 'Perhaps we could look at it now and thrash out some ideas together?'

Fern walked over to the window of the room he had chosen. The scene outside was one of pastoral serenity, a drift of newly shorn white sheep were wandering across the paddock, heading, she guessed, for the dam. For a moment she envied him the outlook.

'I didn't realise you actually farmed here.'

'Oh I don't!' Alex repudiated the idea with a snort of derision. 'I don't mind living in the bush, part time, I certainly don't want to live off it. No, we lease the grazing out to neighbouring farmers, an excellent arrangement, the land brings in an income, albeit small, but requires no effort on my behalf.'

'Of course . . .' she should have known that farming was not quite Alex's scene.

'Fiona had the idea it was good for her image to live on a farm as she is a country singer,' he added as further explanation. 'Good publicity, no doubt, as it will be good publicity for you too, pictures of her home in magazines.'

Fern smiled. 'I was brought up on a farm.' For a moment her eyes held a dreamy look as she remembered her golden childhood.

'Really?' The surprise in his voice was, she knew, a compliment. 'Then you are the very person to ensure the authentic country look.'

'You want this room to look authentic too?' Fern asked with a smile. She was looking at the functional but rather ugly computer station.

'Well, yes, I guess I do, but I have to have somewhere for my computer,' he told her, following her gaze. 'This is, after all, a working study.'

'A pine desk would serve just as well as that.' She grimaced slightly as she indicated the existing workspace. 'Probably better, it has drawers where you can keep paper, disks and things. As you use a laptop you have plenty of room for both that and the printer on the top and maybe a small side table or something for the scanner?' She looked down at the carpet and almost shuddered. It was patterned all over in what must have been a most lurid floral motif when new. The years had toned down the colours somewhat but even so it made the room look small and cramped.

'I would suggest a plain carpet, so much easier to see dropped paperclips on, in a natural fibre, wool, sisal or something, in a nice earth tone or maybe green, what do you think?'

'I take your point about a plain coloured carpet. It took me half the morning to find a two dollar coin, much more serious than a paperclip. It was completely lost in this

197

atrocious pattern.' He shrugged ruefully. 'I eventually had to resort to lying on my side so that I could see it sticking up above the surface.'

Fern was amused at the picture in her mind of Alex prone on the floor hunting down a recalcitrant coin. 'Well, there you are—what colour would you prefer?'

He paced across the small room, giving his attention to this weighty matter. 'Green I think, but not a bright shade, a soft mossy colour with plenty of blue in it, earthy like you said, but at the same time restful.'

'And likely to bring about a state of hypnosis?' Fern remarked and immediately could have bitten her tongue for bringing up the one subject she had no wish to discuss with Alex. 'Drapes, furnishings, wall colour etc., are you happy to leave all that to me?' she hurried on in a more businesslike voice.

'Absolutely,' he agreed. 'Just so long as you run the final design past me, and give me a rough idea of the overall cost.'

'But of course.' That was the way she always worked.

They returned to the kitchen cum dining area and Fern looked around, as Alex took various cling wrapped plates and dishes from the fridge. She felt a thrill of pleasure, of achievement, the room was so very different from the old-fashioned inconvenient kitchen she had first seen, and in fact it was totally unrecognisable. But this intimate dinner for two was not at all what she had expected.

Watching Alex uncork a bottle of chilled chardonnay, she thought how striking his classic features and tall graceful body were, and those vivid blue eyes must be quite an asset in a hypnotist. He asked how her book was going, and whether she had a publisher lined up for it.

'Sort of—a friend who is a book editor actually gave me the idea. So if I get it finished I should have a toe in, but at the moment it isn't progressing much.'

'I suppose you are too busy doing up houses for city people seeking refuge in the country,' Alex suggested with a smile. 'Are you taking on the Stones' cottage, by the way?'

Fern nodded. 'Yes—I'm quite looking forward to it. Do you know them?'

'Oh yes—Mandy and Fiona were at boarding school together. Mandy's parents have a property in this area and Fiona used to visit—that is why she likes the district. Miles' parents also have a wheat and wool place round here, he and Mandy were childhood sweethearts.' He smiled as if he found this more amusing than romantic.

'So you could say they are both the genuine article.' Hearing her own words, Fern hoped Alex would not think she was criticising him and Fiona. 'What does Miles do for a crust?' she asked.

'He is a would-be artist . . .' Fern noticed the slight stress on the 'would-be', 'and helps his parents and in-laws out as required.'

The conversation had flowed easily back and forth as they ate, and the level in the wine bottle had dropped steadily, Fern realised she was both relaxed and enjoying herself. She asked Alex about his book, and though she thought some of his ideas way out, others she found interesting.

'I expect you think I lured you here by yourself so that I could be sure of no interruptions while I sent you off into the land of never-never?' There was a sardonic twist in his smile as he passed her coffee.

'Not at all,' Fern replied primly, although that was exactly what she had thought at the beginning of the evening.

'I had no idea we would be on our own till Fiona told me that she was going up to Melbourne with Paul.'

'With Paul?' To Fern, her voice seemed to come out as a sort of peeved croak.

'Yes—it was a spur of the moment thing as far as Fiona was concerned, when Paul told her he couldn't come tonight because he had to go to Melbourne she took the opportunity to go with him.'

'Oh.' Fern couldn't think of anything to say that wouldn't give away her feelings, predominant at the moment a quite malevolent dislike of Alex—for telling her.

Common sense reminded her that shooting the messenger who brought bad tidings was a totally pointless and primitive reaction. She forced herself to look directly at him and smile; she certainly wasn't going to let him think she was concerned. Meeting his eyes she had the disconcerting impression that he had enjoyed telling her.

Still smiling, although she could feel her lips stiffening, she said, glancing at her watch, 'I guess I had better be making tracks myself. Thank you for a pleasant evening, I'll get some ideas down on paper and let you have them.' She half expected him to try and detain her on some pretext or other, but to her surprise, he merely held his hand out.

'We'll shake on that. I certainly like your suggestions.' As he released her hand he turned and led the way to the door. Irrationally, Fern felt disappointed that he was letting her go so easily.

CHAPTER NINE

Fern booted up her computer as soon as she got home in an effort to replace Paul in her thoughts. She put in her ideas for Alex's sanctum as she had outlined it to him and only when she had fixed it up to her satisfaction, did she go to bed. All it needed now was Alex's seal of approval and she could get the work under way. Doing this had kept Paul in the background, but when she switched off the bedside light, he crept insidiously back. Why hadn't either he or Fiona mentioned they were going to Melbourne together? Perhaps Alex was right and it had been a sudden decision on Fiona's part. But did that make it any better, or did it merely show that Fiona was on such good terms with him that she could do that sort of thing?

Her body ached for him as she vainly chased sleep and she remembered the last time they had made love. Had it been as good for him as it had for her? Maybe she had disappointed him, her fear of getting emotionally involved again put him off? Or had he just not found her as irresistible as she did him? She tormented herself with thoughts that buzzed in her head like bees.

She had left Melbourne full of good resolutions to put the pain of her old life behind her and to steer clear of any new relationship that threatened to become too close, but she hadn't bargained on meeting Paul, who had proven both a fantastic lover and a good friend. Her last thought, however, was not of him, but Alex. Wondering if, maybe—just maybe, he could help her sort out her life, both waking and sleeping, into some semblance of order, she fell asleep.

If she dreamed, she did not remember.

Fern was still sipping her first coffee of the day and Boss his milk, when the phone rang. She snatched up the receiver, maybe it was Paul. She did her best not to sound disappointed when she recognised Mandy Stone's voice.

'I wondered if you had time to call round and check on progress?' The Stones were doing most of the actual work of re-decorating their cottage themselves following Fern's guidelines.

'Sure—I'd love to!' her enthusiastic response sounded hollow in her own ears. 'This morning?'

'Terrific! Come any time.'

Fern dropped the receiver in its cradle with a slight sigh. At least it would be hard to mope about Paul in their company, for they were both full of enthusiasm for their project. She was busy sorting out her notes and cramming anything she might need into her briefcase when she heard a car door slam and footsteps approaching her door. He was still knocking when she flung it open.

'Hi!' Paul greeted her.

'Hi!' Fern strove for normalcy. 'Have a good trip?' she managed not to add, 'with Fiona'.

'Yes, thanks. Sorry about last night—did you enjoy the evening?' He stepped inside and asked, 'Any coffee going?'

'Oh—just a quick one. I am off to the Stones'. They just called asking if I could go and inspect work in progress—their work—they are doing most of it themselves.' Fern switched the jug on to re-heat. 'Why don't you come too?' she suggested a few moments later as she placed two mugs of coffee in front of them.

'I think I will,' he agreed as if making a momentous decision. 'My horoscope mentioned "unexpected invitations" today.' He was bending down to stroke Boss so Fern was unable to see if he were serious.

'I suppose you check on your stars every day?'

'Yep! First thing I look at in the paper—before I check on my shares even.' Fern suspected he was teasing, but when he said, 'I saw a tarot reader last night,' he seemed perfectly serious.

'You what?' He had all her attention now and Fern could not have been more amazed if he had confessed to the most heinous crime.

'Did I hear you right?' was all she could think of to say. She looked at him, wondering, 'Does believing in that sort of thing make you happy?'

'Does not believing make you happy?' he countered.

Fern was non-committal. 'Tell me then, about this tarot reader. Did she predict a brilliant future?'

'Absolutely. And a gorgeous auburn haired drop-in from the sixteenth century to share it with me.'

'You are laughing at me. I don't believe you did anything of the sort.' Remembering he had not been alone she asked, her voice sharper than she intended, 'Did Fiona go with you?'

'She was there.'

'Oh.' There seemed nothing else to say.

After a pause in which Fern sat miserably chewing her lip, he smiled, leaned slightly toward her and explained. 'I called Fiona to tell her I couldn't get there for dinner as I had to go to Melbourne. She said she was about to ring me herself as she had just heard that this friend of hers, who just happens to read the tarot cards, had been taken to hospital after an accident. She is rather a wonderful old lady and Fiona thinks the world of her, so . . . I offered her a lift.'

'I see . . . but why couldn't Alex have told me that?' she demanded.

Paul's shoulders lifted in that slight—and so expressive—shrug that expressed without words that he didn't know, and anyway did it matter? 'Fiona said she tried to get hold of you but your phone was engaged and your mobile turned off. And anyway it was Alex who really wanted to see you.'

'Oh,' Fern said lamely, 'I was on the internet probably and my mobile was turned off so that I wouldn't be distracted. I forgot to check my messages.' After a moment's silence, she added, 'Do you know Fiona's friend?'

'Yes—very well, I owe a lot to her,' Paul continued, quite serious now. 'She showed me that life could be worth living even when you were sure it was not.' He was silent for a few minutes as if reviewing that time, then added, 'She sparked my interest in reincarnation.'

'Oh,' Fern repeated, wishing she could think of something more intelligent to say than this pathetic monosyllable. She thought of their first meeting, his finger tilting her face to his, and the caress in his voice when he said, 'You *haven't changed.*' She glanced at her watch. 'If we are going to the Stones' . . . I did say I would be there almost immediately.'

Paul consulted his own watch. 'Is that the time? I didn't realise it was getting so late. I think I will have to pass on this unexpected invitation after all, I have things to do, folks to see.' He moved across to the door. 'Thanks for the coffee, I'll be seeing you around, I guess.' And with that, he was gone.

Fern watched the door close behind him with a sharp stab of anger. He had touched her core somehow, made her feel quite emotional. Then he went—just like that. And she, dammit, was seared with jealousy of Fiona who seemed to know him so well, and who had spent the whole evening—longer for all she knew—with him. Grabbing up all the things she needed, or might need, at the Stones', she snatched up her car keys and slammed out of the house.

'How are you finding life in the bush after the big smoke?' Miles asked in his bushman's drawl as he and Fern sat at the rustic garden setting while Mandy made coffee. 'Not too dull for you?'

'Oh, no. I like it, it's just great,' Fern assured him. 'The pace is so restful and the people so friendly, I feel I am on one long vacation.'

Miles' smile was a touch sardonic. 'You must miss city life?' he persisted.

'I'm not dependent on it,' Fern told him. 'I was raised in rural Tasmania.' She thought for a moment, then added, 'I miss the pressure at times, whatever it was that kept the adrenaline pumping, but I don't feel lonely here.' She smiled up at Mandy, carrying a tray loaded with steaming coffee and freshly baked scones. Fern looked at them appreciatively, suddenly hungry.

'I have a few suggestions for this place,' Fern said, licking melted butter from her finger. The scones were still warm. 'You are a good cook,' she told Mandy.

'We have too,' Mandy replied. 'Ideas I mean. I wanted to throw them at you and see what you thought.'

Fern pulled her coffee towards her. 'Fire away!'

'Well . . .' Mandy began hesitantly as if wondering whether it was up to her to give advice or make suggestions to the expert they had called in to tell them. Miles had no such compunction.

'This area here,' he supplied for her, 'it's fine when the weather is just right, that is not too hot, not too cold and not raining, but we thought how much better it would be if we had a sort of outdoor room here that we could use in all weather.'

Fern looked around the paved area where they were sitting at the rustic garden setting; pleasant enough but very ordinary and, as Miles had pointed out, only functional in optimal conditions. Turning the area into an outdoor/indoor living area was a good one, and something that she should have thought of herself. That, after all, was what they were paying her for.

'You mean enclose it?' she asked. To Mandy's nod she continued, 'Were you thinking of a veranda, just put a lid over this area, or were you thinking more on the lines of enclose it and actually making another room?'

'A lid would be an improvement . . .' Mandy said hesitantly.

'But it still wouldn't turn it into an all-weather area,' Miles pointed out. 'If we are going to do anything, we should enclose it.'

'A conservatory?' Fern suggested.

Mandy smiled. 'That sounds rather grand for an old cottage like this. I was thinking more on the lines of an all purpose garden room, a sunroom if you like, somewhere to laze and relax, entertain informally . . .' she

208

trailed off and looked expectantly at Fern. 'I'm sure you know what I mean?'

Thus appealed to, Fern switched fully into professional mode. She got up and paced the grey pavers in front of the house where the table and chairs stood. A very small veranda offered minimal protection from the weather. She looked up and it was suddenly clear as crystal what to do. 'Suppose we remove or extend that pitiful bit up there for starters,' she pointed upwards, 'and bring the roof outwards to about here,' she moved back several large steps. 'We'll use tinted laminated glass for that so that we don't block any light from the house, it also cuts out about ninety-five percent of ultra violet rays, change these dreary pavers for terracotta tiling or something. Have glass or aluminium trellis for the walls, or a blend, fill with pot plants, and there you are—a sun room in winter, add some blinds and you have a shade room in summer.' She stopped suddenly, aware that she had been carried away by her own ideas, and looked anxiously at her hosts, but Mandy was beaming happily.

'I was sure you would come up with some good ideas.'

Miles, more restrained, said, 'Sounds as if it might work, I'd like to see some plans on paper, and have a rough idea of cost.'

Fern tuned in to a popular music station on her car radio and found herself humming along with it as she drove home. She had not expected to get any commissions out here in the country, or meet such interesting and enthusiastic people. As she outlined her ideas to the Stones, the idea for a piece for one of the glossies she wrote for took root in her mind. She would call it, 'Creating a Garden Room'.

'Oh damn!' she cursed softly to herself when she saw Alex's white Saab drawn up at her front gate. What did he want now? She knew she wouldn't have felt so irritated if it had been Paul's car standing there.

He stepped out of the car as she drew up in her short driveway. As she switched off the engine and opened her own door she heard the decisive slam of his car door and turned to face him. She could see he was annoyed.

'I have been waiting for nearly an hour.' He looked tight-lipped and sounded terse.

'I'm sorry,' Fern said, then turned back to the car to collect her laptop and papers. 'If I had known you were coming . . .' she went on in what she hoped was a soothing voice as she backed out of the car.

'You did know,' he interrupted her, 'I said I was looking forward to seeing what you came up with for my den . . .'

'Yes, I know you did, but you didn't say you were coming round today.' Neither, she could have added, did I say I would have them ready.

Alex shrugged. 'Well, I'm here.'

Fern bit off a sharp retort and contented herself with a mild, 'Yes.' He was following her up the garden path now and she had little alternative but to add, 'Come in, anyway, and if you have changed your mind about anything we'll go through it again.'

He was looking at his watch as he waited for her to unlock the door. 'To tell you the truth, I would much rather take you out to lunch than work out colour schemes . . . I'm quite happy with the suggestions you made yesterday.' Surprised by his invitation Fern turned to face the full barrage of his charm. 'What do you say—how about it?'

'Well, thank you,' she accepted politely like an obedient child being reminded of its Ps & Qs, 'that would be nice.'

Seated opposite him in the restaurant, Fern wondered what was behind his visit and invitation, and then immediately asked herself why she should imagine there was anything behind it. She soon got her answer. 'When are you going to feel up to another session?' Alex asked.

'Another session?' Fern stalled. With more work on hand, she wasn't sure she wanted to spare the time. 'You didn't tell me Fiona went to Melbourne to see someone in hospital.'

'Didn't I?' Alex replied blandly. 'Should I have done?'

Fern did not have an answer. 'Paul mentioned that she read tarot cards . . .' Fern

211

wasn't quite sure why she brought this up, but in the face of Alex's silence, she felt compelled to carry on. 'How can anyone look at a few cards and tell you anything helpful or relevant?'

'They think they can.' It was an ambiguous answer.

'Paul says she helped him.' Why couldn't she drop the subject?

'He thinks she did, if that is what he feels then she probably did. It's all in the mind, you know, Fern.' She thought, and almost said, that was just what a psychologist would say, but before she had a chance to make a suitable reply, Alex went on, rather testily. 'I didn't ask you to lunch just to discuss Paul and his problems. When will you feel up to having another session with me and doing something about your own?'

'I don't want you putting all the stupid things I say in your book,' Fern protested.

'You are putting my house in yours,' he reminded her.

'That, if I may so, is quite different.'

'Why?'

'Well, a house is—just a house. But I am me, I'm a person.' Surely he could see the difference.

'And the house is our home, and, as such, part of us, of me and Fiona.' Suddenly he leaned across the table and dropped his hand lightly on her arm and smiled. 'Not to worry, you can say what you like, in fact I think Fiona would be mortified if you failed to say whose house it was, good publicity for her you know.'

'If I agree, promise not to mention my name in your book?' Fern persisted, conscious that his fingers had rested just a shade too long on her bare arm.

'Okay—okay. I'll only refer to you as case B or whatever.'

Fern pushed her plate to one side. 'This afternoon?' she suggested, might as well bite the bullet and get it over and done with. 'You said Paul had problems—what did you mean?'

Alex didn't answer immediately, then, 'If he hasn't told you himself then I don't think I should,' was all he said.

Fern shrugged. 'Guess not.' She picked up her coffee cup feeling rebuffed by Alex and somewhat hurt that Paul had not confided in her. Suddenly, she realised how very little he had ever said about himself, less even than she had revealed to him about her own life. But then, why should he? Her voice was cool as she said, 'Well, Alex, if I am to give up my afternoon to be your case study, let's get on with it.' She gave him a level look before adding, 'Your place or mine?'

CHAPTER TEN

Fern felt marginally more comfortable in her own home, so she pointed out to Alex that as his room was about to be re-designed it would be more sensible to have this session at her cottage. 'Also . . .' she added, 'as we are so much nearer my place than yours it will save time.'

'But I haven't got my CD player,' he complained. Fern offered the use of her own. He produced a small voice activated taperecorder, and his folder of notes and she wondered aloud if he always went out to lunch equipped to do an on the spot hypnosis session.

'Who said anything about hypnosis?'

Fern was sceptical, but merely shrugged and pulled a wry face.

'You appeared to enjoy it.'

'I wouldn't go as far as that. Let's just say it was more pleasant than I expected. Or less unpleasant,' she corrected, settling herself in her own most comfortable armchair.

Fern leaned back in the chair, her hands resting on the arms. She stretched her legs out on the footrest. God, but she was tired. She yawned and closed her eyes. 'A rest would be pleasant anyway,' was her last conscious thought as the soft rhythmic thrum of the disk

Alex was playing enveloped her . . .

'Elizabeth, Elizabeth!' Her stomach clenched as she heard her name called. He only used her full name when he was annoyed or issuing a command, or both. That was most of the time these days, it seemed an age since he had used the diminutive, Beth. She was glad he had never called her Liz, that had been her father's pet name for her: now there was only one person in the world who ever called her that.

'Elizabeth!' the voice came as an angry roar now. With a sigh, a tightening of her lips and a nervous glance at her maid, she put down her needlework and moved out of the room onto the balcony that overlooked the great hall. The stiff taffeta of her dress rustled as she walked.

She moved to the heavy oak banister that ran along the balcony and followed the wide curving stairway down into the hall itself. She dropped her hands on the polished wood and looked down. She tensed automatically as her eyes went straight to the stocky figure of her husband, foreshortened by the angle at which she looked down on him. He was looking straight up at her and even from this distance she could see the glint of triumph in his eyes. Fear, cold and clammy, touched her and her hands tightened on the wooden balustrade until the knuckles blanched, she did not speak, afraid that a tremor in her voice might betray her.

Up to this point the memory was just as she had dreamed it so many times before, but as she looked down the faces below, that of her husband and of the man on the bier, swam in and out of focus. As they settled, she saw with horror that the face she was used to seeing was not Nigel's, but the man she now knew as Alex Cameron, or was it? Even as she recognised him, his features once more swam in and out of focus and when they settled it was the face of her husband, or the man who had been her husband recently. Aware of a terrifying dichotomy in her self or a merging, she couldn't be sure which, it was as if her consciousness was in two places, two time frames and two people at the same time. She put her fist to her mouth in a futile effort to stop the screaming, it was no good, the sound was inside and outside her, beating at her senses and at the same time tearing at her very soul.

As she stared down at the face of the dead man, it changed before her eyes and became Paul. As she stood there, she was conscious of the most terrible searing pain sweeping through her. Grief for the man lying on the stretcher was the greatest component, but mingled with it was that icy fear inspired by the other man who she knew as her husband. She had expected to recognise Nigel but now he seemed to have Alex's face, or did he, the image was swimming in and out of focus as he smiled at her with a triumphant malevolence, was he boasting of killing, or was he accusing her? She could not tell, she only knew that she was filled with a *deadly chilling fear. With a soft moan she loosed her hold on the oak railing and in a rustle and murmur of crumpled silk, fell to the floor . . .*

As Fern opened her eyes, the echo of her screams died away. She put a shaking hand up to her face; it came away damp from the tears on her cheeks. To her immense relief, she could feel the dream, or whatever it was, slipping away to the extent that she even wondered why she seemed so upset. She looked up and saw Alex watching her. For a wild moment, she imagined his face still had the same look of malevolent triumph it had worn in her dream, but even as a shudder ran through her, he smiled and it was the urbane charming Alex she knew. She shook her head, and immediately regretted the action as it seemed to start twin hammers in her temples. She tried to remember why Alex was here.

'Sorry, Fern, that was a bit rough.'

She wondered what he meant and why he was saying he was sorry when he was looking anything but. On the contrary, he was looking as self-satisfied as the proverbial cat with the cream. She closed her eyes to try and recollect where she had been, what she had been doing, above all to recall what had upset her so much. Her eye fell on the taperecorder and it came back, Alex had been conducting some bizarre experiment with her mind in an attempt to prove some theory of his about the ability of people to remember, and return to, past lives.

217

'You programmed me to forget, didn't you?' she accused as she struggled to a sitting position, shaking her head as she did so then putting her fingers up to her temples in an attempt to still the dull throbbing. 'You've got it all there on that thing,' she indicated the cassette recorder, 'but you don't particularly want me to remember, do you?'

'Come now, Fern, you credit me with greater powers than I have, but of course, it would not be fair of me to upset you when you have been so helpful in my project.' He smiled as he took the audio tape out of his small portable taperecorder and slipped it in his pocket. 'I could not expect you to continue helping me if you found it too unpleasant. Now—I think a cup of tea would be in order.'

'Yes of course.' Fern sat up straight and let her legs swing over the side of the chair, some dim memory reminded her that Alex should be obeyed.

He held up a restraining hand. 'No—no, stay where you are. I will make it.' Thankfully, Fern dropped back in her chair and closed her eyes, the thought flitting through her mind that she was paying a high price for the privilege of writing up a before and after story featuring the Camerons' house.

She voiced this thought when Alex brought the promised tea.

'You know, it has just occurred to me that you are getting a better deal out of this than I am. Publicity for your house can be nothing but an asset to you, certainly for Fiona, but I feel my credibility as a sane and responsible interior designer would plummet if it was reported that I was undergoing "past life therapy", or whatever name this goes by.' She refrained from adding that not only was she sceptical about the past life bit but not at all convinced that these sessions were therapeutic. She hadn't the slightest recollection of what she had dreamed, yet she had referred to it so glibly as 'past life' therapy? Fern frowned slightly to herself and was thoughtful as she sipped the hot sweet tea Alex handed to her.

'Do you want to remember?' he asked her now.

'I don't know, I really don't. If they are anything like the dreams I have been having lately, I think not. She leaned her head back and closed her eyes briefly.

'Why don't you tell me about your dreams?' Alex suggested, his voice soft, almost caressing. 'After all, they are what is troubling you, they are the reason that you agreed to these sessions in the first place, aren't they?'

'Paul suggested it . . .' she began. 'Did he tell you about the dreams?' her voice had a sharp edge before she floundered into silence. She realised that she was giving away far more about her relationship with Paul than she wanted Alex, or anyone, to know.

He was looking at her now with that irritating half smile on his lips. It was the expression on his face as much as the realisation that Paul had betrayed her confidence that made her voice steely. 'I am sure you have gleaned quite enough information in the last twenty minutes or so to keep you going for a while. My dreams, good or bad, can remain my own property.'

'But Fern,' Alex protested, 'my book is about dreams.'

'Then why all this past life stuff?'

'I thought I had explained, I have this theory—we access our past lives in dreams. Some of us anyway.'

'You think that is what I am doing?' In spite of herself, Fern was interested.

'I do—and I am sure I could help you.'

'What makes you so sure I need help?'

Alex shrugged. 'Most of us do—one way or another.'

'How comforting for you,' Fern could not resist saying, 'as a clinical psychologist in private practice, to have so many potential clients.'

A spasm of annoyance crossed his face, he pushed away his teacup, and rose to his feet, saying in his usual urbane manner, 'And now my dear Fern, I must love you and leave you, I have things to do.'

'And so do I,' she retorted somewhat brusquely. She could see that she had annoyed him. Well that was just too bad, she was heartily sick of all this nonsense. The only life she was interested in was the one she was living right now.

After he left, she returned to her computer searching for the files of articles that she could put together to make the book she planned. Totally absorbed in her work, she was unhampered by past problems or painful memories surfacing to distract her.

When she finally closed down her computer more than a couple of hours later she felt stuffy and housebound. She glanced across at Boss peacefully asleep in his favourite chair. Somehow he had managed to insinuate himself into becoming a house cat, and wished that he were a dog to give her the excuse to walk. She squashed the thought immediately, she was perfectly able to walk without that excuse.

She pulled on a light parka, the sky had turned grey and a slight wind had risen, changed her shoes and set off determinedly for the relatively open country beyond the little township. Walking was something she had done very little of since she had left the city. Curiously enough, she had done much more there, albeit mostly in the city parks, but then Bubbles had given her a reason. As she strode out heading away from town, she took deep breaths of air, realising how she had missed this cheapest and simplest of all forms of exercise. She was a good twenty minutes away from home when the grey sky turned black, with what seemed amazing suddenness, there was an ominous rumble and then the heavens opened.

Her first instinct was to seek protection, but recalling the many stories she had heard of people being struck by lightning sheltering under trees, Fern moved out from the haven of the large gum she had instinctively sought and strode firmly back to the township. Within seconds, the heavy rain had penetrated her light parachute nylon parka, her jeans were clinging to her like a second skin, her hair was hanging in rats' tails around her face and her shoes made an unpleasant squelch with each step she took. Head bent against the onslaught of the ferocious rain, she strode doggedly toward home.

She was more than three quarters of the way there when a car overtook her, braked suddenly and reversed back at high speed to stop beside her. The window slid down and Paul leaned across the passenger seat. 'Good God, woman, what on earth are you doing?' He pulled open the door. 'Get in before you drown.'

'But I'm soaked—your car . . .' Fern protested without much conviction.

'Never mind the car, just get in,' he ordered. Fern obeyed, repressing a shiver and trying not to notice the way she was dripping onto the floor and soaking the sheepskin cover on the seat.

'Do you enjoy walking in the rain?'

'It wasn't raining when I set out, I just wanted to well—walk—get out in the fresh air; I . . .' she trailed off with a shrug, annoyed with herself for the stammering explanation she was giving, as if she were a guilty schoolgirl.

'Hrrumph,' Paul made a non-committal noise that could have meant anything or nothing as he drew the car to a halt at her gate.

Fern clambered out and was sticking her head back in the car, but he too was out in the rain. 'You don't have to . . .' she began then snapped her mouth shut and slammed the car door as she realised she was only talking to his retreating back. She squelched up the path behind him as fast as she could, fumbling for her door key in the pocket of her sodden parka as she ran. 'You don't need . . .' she began again as she fitted her key in the lock.

'No, I don't,' was his uncompromising answer, 'but I'm coming in to make sure you take care of yourself properly.'

Fern's first reaction was to turn on him angrily, but she just shrugged and said nothing. She could hardly tell him not to come in when he had just rescued her. She shivered as she closed the door behind them.

'Go and get some dry things on, I'll put the jug on for a warm drink.' Paul's tone made it clear that argument was not an option.

'Make yourself at home,' she meant to sound sarcastic, but her chattering teeth rather spoilt the effect. She headed for a hot shower and dry clothes.

Twenty minutes later, warm and dry, with her hair roughly towelled, she re-joined Paul in the kitchen. Cups were on the table, he had even found some biscuits, and the jug was hot. 'Tea or coffee?' he asked.

'Er, tea, thanks.' How, she wondered, had she, who prided herself on her independence, allowed herself to be in a position to have soothing tea made for her, not once but twice in one day and not even by the same man at that? She watched Paul pouring the hot water into the pot, for a moment she felt she had seen him doing this simple action many times before. She dismissed the thought as absurd as she reached her hand out for the steaming mug he was pushing across the table to her.

'A penny for them?' he said as he had once before.

'They aren't worth that even, just a moment of, I suppose what you would call, déjà vu.' She spoke lightly, dismissing her remark, or trying to, with a smile and a shrug. Paul was not so easily diverted.

'You too are beginning to think we have met before?'

'No—I didn't say that,' she protested, while at the same time not at all sure just what she did mean. 'It's just that . . . Oh, I don't know . . .'

she floundered helplessly, 'in dreams perhaps?' She had meant to sound ironic, even scathing. To her dismay, she only succeeded in sounding wistful.

Paul, as she might have guessed, answered her seriously. 'Could be—but whose dreams, yours or mine, or both?'

Maybe it was the feeling of being securely cocooned in the little kitchen together while the storm still raged outside, but Fern found herself admitting as she held her warm mug in both hands, 'Well, mine I suppose, I can't claim to know anything about yours.'

'Is it permissible to ask how I appear in your dreams?'

Fern peered down into her mug, rather than directly at him, her lips twisted into a wry smile. 'Dead,' she answered succinctly with a slight shrug.

'Oh, am I. Was I very dead?'

Fern nodded. 'And it seems to be my fault in some way.'

'You mean you killed me?'

'Oh, no! But I feel that it is my fault somehow that you are dead, so I feel guilty, but worse than that—along with the guilt is a terrible fear.' She shuddered involuntarily. 'It is this dread, absolute terror, that makes me wake up.'

'And I thought it was just seeing me dead.'

'That too,' Fern began seriously before looking up and seeing that Paul, while serious, was not entirely so. 'Oh—I wish I hadn't told you.' She began to push her chair back from the table but, with a swift movement, Paul leaned across and caught hold of her wrist.

'I'm sorry,' he said, 'sorry that you have these nightmares and sorry too that I seem to be the cause of them, however unwittingly. Please, will you tell me more?'

'Well, there is not much to tell really. It's always the same, well till last time. It seems to be the sixteenth century or thereabouts, it starts pleasantly enough, I'm in my room, sewing, with my maid. Someone calls my name, I put down the sewing and walk out of my room onto a balcony that overlooks the main hall of what appears to be a large country house in Herefordshire or Worcestershire, somewhere in that region . . .'

'How do you know where it is?' Paul interrupted.

Fern looked at him, how did she know? 'I just—know,' she snapped. 'Don't interrupt if you want me to tell you.' She frowned, willing herself back into the dream. 'I am wearing a plum coloured dress of some stiff silk material, it rustles as I walk, it has cream lace at the wrists and around the high neck. I walk to the heavy balustrade and with my hands resting on it, no not resting, gripping it, very tightly, I look down into the hall. Two men in the rough clothes of farm labourers are carrying a sort of improvised stretcher, it's a gate, or a hurdle or something, another—person—is standing there looking up. It is this man who called my name, when he sees me he pulls the cover off the body on the stretcher and I see . . .' she paused and her voice dropped to a whisper, 'that it is you. I feel such pain I think I must faint, but I know I must not betray my feelings. I grip the railing so tightly, my knuckles are white, and, and . . .' Her voice trailed off and when she looked at Paul across the table, her eyes swam and she felt a choking feeling in her chest and throat, the same feeling she always had in the dream.

'And?' His voice was quiet but with a ring of command, she knew she had to answer.

'This is the really terrible bit . . . I deny him—you. I say I have never seen you before, even ask why I am being shown this—body. I turn away and, summoning all the self-control at my disposal, walk back to my room. But I am cold, and shaking with both grief and a terrible deadly fear. That is the moment when I wake up.'

'What makes you so afraid, or who are you so afraid of?' Paul asked quietly.

'I don't know,' Fern answered swiftly. Too swiftly. She felt herself flushing slightly under Paul's silent scrutiny. 'The man calling me, making me look at—the body,' she finally mumbled.

'Do you know him, I mean recognise him as someone you know in this life?' Paul persisted.

Fern nodded, even now forcing herself to remember she felt the familiar fear and dread of the dream.

'Can you tell me?'

Fern nodded. 'My husband, usually.' So much she could say. Somehow it sounded too bizarre to say that the last dream had been more terrifying than usual, because the place of her dead husband had been taken over temporarily by Alex.

Paul quickly picked her up on that hesitant last word. 'Usually, you mean it isn't always?'

She jumped to her feet, almost knocking over her chair in her haste. 'Look—I don't want to talk about it any more. My husband is dead, in the dream he is alive, you are alive, in the dream you are dead. In real life you never even met one another as far as I know, the whole thing is just absurd, ridiculous, too bizarre for words. I don't want to even think about it.' Hearing the shrill, almost hysterical, note in her rising voice, Fern took a deep breath, consciously trying to speak calmly and rationally. 'It's a dream—a rather silly dream that's all, and I am rather silly too to be bothered by it.'

'Fair enough,' Paul could see she was having trouble keeping a grip on herself. 'But I don't understand how Alex comes into it.'

'He doesn't. What I am trying to explain to you is the weird way I seemed to be in two places at once. It—it was like . . .' She sought

228

frantically for the right words, 'as if I have been anaesthetised, but not quite enough. I am still aware of what's going on. That is the nearest I can get to describe it. Look, Paul, I don't really want to think any more about this,' she said. 'The whole thing is so bizarre it makes me think I can't be normal—whatever that is.'

'The ability to work and love—according to Freud anyway,' Paul murmured.

'You sound like a psychologist,' Fern remarked dryly. 'Anyway, we've talked enough about me, what about you?'

'Thank you, but, no. My apologies if you feel I have invaded your inner privacy. Fern could feel him distancing himself, or pushing her away. She felt she had upset him, but wasn't sure how. He glanced towards the window. 'The storm seems spent, I think I could reach my car without a drenching.'

'Thanks for rescuing me.' She watched him walk to the door, there was so much more she wanted to say to him. She waited for him to turn and bid her 'Goodbye'.

He turned, but all he said was, 'Don't worry—*you* are quite normal.'

'Paul . . .' her voice sounded weak and she was uncomfortably aware of a slight quaver, but totally unaware that she held out one hand in a gesture of supplication. With a click of finality the door closed behind him. Swiftly, she crossed to the window. Beyond the rain soaked front garden, she could see he had already reached his car. Within seconds, he was gone. She stood for a moment staring bleakly at the spot where his car had stood, wondering at her feeling of helplessness and guilt. Then it came to her, this was how she felt in her dream when she was forced to gaze down on his body, but the griping fear had gone, leaving merely a deep sense of unease.

Fern tried to draw comfort from the fact that Paul had at least classed her as normal. Maybe, but not sensible or she would not have embarked on this absurd agreement with Alex. But it was not in her nature to renege on a promise.

It was, however, with very mixed feelings that she fronted up for her next session. To her relief, Fiona opened the door to her. The younger girl always seemed so genuinely pleased to see her and so cheerful that just meeting her smile cleared away some of the dark shadows from Fern's mind.

'Hi, come right in!' Fiona flung the door wide with an expansive grin that warmed Fern's heart and allayed her fears.

A welcoming smell of freshly brewed coffee filled the air. 'I saw your car draw up and as I had the jug boiling I poured the water into the coffee plunger,' Fiona told her, leading the way into the kitchen. A pleasant smell of baking also filled the air and Fern was surprised to see a wire tray of cooling scones on the table. She hadn't associated home cooking with Fiona who, as if guessing her thoughts, added, 'I'm quite domestic now I have this wonderful kitchen to be domestic in.' Then with disarming candour, 'Actually they are made with a packet mix, but it is a start.'

Indicating a chair at the table and placing a plate and knife in front of Fern, she turned to the fridge and pulled out a carton of butter and a plastic bottle of milk. 'Try one,' she said as she pushed down the plunger in the coffee pot and filled two mugs before flopping down in the chair on the opposite side of the table.

For a few moments they munched and sipped in silence. 'Mmmm—not bad, considering,' Fern murmured.

'That they are packet scones or my first ever effort?' Fiona grinned. 'Is this a social visit or are you once more offering yourself up on the altar of Alex's study of the power of one mind, his, on another, yours?'

Fern did not like this interpretation of her arrangement with Alex, maybe because it seemed rather too near the truth to be comfortable. 'We have a mutually beneficial arrangement,' she answered rather stiffly. 'I help him in his research for his book and he gives me permission to feature this house in articles and in a book I am trying to put together.'

Fiona's answering snort of derision was somewhat muted by the large bite of scone she had just taken. She chewed and swallowed. 'Actually the house is mine, and as a relative newcomer to the entertainment scene, publicity, even for the house not me, would be welcome. So it would seem that the real beneficiary of this little exercise is me. Of course, if you help Alex to prove whatever it is he is trying to prove, then he will be delighted. I suppose if you get some real help and possibly enjoyment, it will be worth it for you, too. But on the face of it, I would say I am the one to benefit most.'

'Yes, I suppose so.' What else was there to say? She drained her coffee and pushed back her chair wondering where Alex was and why he was not here having coffee with them.

'Alex is in his den, he declined coffee, said he didn't want caffeine interfering with his concentration.' Fiona's tone was sceptical. 'You'd better go along I suppose, unless you would like another cup?'

Fern shook her head. 'No—thanks, that was lovely and the scones were nice. Though I feel a bit guilty, I didn't give the caffeine a thought. I suppose I had better go along.'

'Of course you didn't, you are far too sensible. But yes—you had better run along— or he will be hunting you up.'

She found Alex in the recliner chair where he usually placed her, his eyes closed, listening to the music playing softly on his CD player. For a moment Fern thought of backing out and closing the door behind her, but even while the idea flitted across her mind, he opened his eyes, sat up and swung his feet to the floor.

'Ah, Fern, you are here. I have a new CD and was checking it out before I play it for you.' His smile was disarming, getting to his feet, he indicated that she should take the chair he had vacated.

Reluctantly, Fern moved forward. She wanted to ask how many more of these sessions he planned, but could not find the words without sounding curt and ungracious. She sat down murmuring a vague query about, 'how was his research going?'

'Good—good!' he told her cheerfully. 'A few more sessions and I think we will be there.'

'There?' Fern managed to ask, wondering to herself where 'there' was. Who was 'we' she also wanted to ask. As far as she was concerned this was Alex's pigeon, she was merely the not so willing tool. Already the music and the familiarity of Alex's voice was having an effect, her lids felt heavy and even saying that one word had been an effort. It was easiest to let go and listen to the voice, follow the directions. He was taking her down a steep stone staircase, step by step. When she reached the bottom his voice told her she would have gone beyond her present existence, she would have gone back in time to an earlier life. With each step down the stone stairs she was moving backwards—backwards in time.

She couldn't tell at which point she became aware of the change in her clothes. Or when she felt and heard the rustle of long skirts about her ankles, but it was somewhere around this point that she consciously slowed down. She didn't want to arrive at her destination—wherever that was. She had an uncomfortable feeling that it would mean precipitation into those painful dreams. Why, she wondered, couldn't she go to a happy point in her life, or lives, there must surely be some?

Even as she thought this, she felt a curious sensation beneath her body. 'I'm sitting on a horse!' she realised.

Fern struggled to open her eyes, all too aware of the steady pounding in her temples. For a moment she could not place the man in the room fiddling with the controls of a taperecorder, then 'Listen!' he commanded and she heard her own voice filling the room with what, at first, seemed incomprehensible rubbish. But as she listened she also remembered.

'I'm sitting on a horse!' she heard herself exclaim. *'Side-saddle, she is fidgeting beneath me, I am trying to make her stand still, I am waiting for someone. I am anxious, it is unlike him to be late, then I see another horse coming along the woodland ride. I recognise the rider, I feel my heart beat faster and my excitement is*

234

communicated to my mount, the fidget becomes a dance.

The man, who is riding a magnificent chestnut horse, sweeps off his plumed hat and inclines his head in a bow. 'Good afternoon Lady Elizabeth!' he greets me.

I nod graciously, 'Good afternoon Sir Rupert!' Laughter is trembling on both our lips as we greet one another so correctly, holding his hat as a screen, he leans forward and kisses me softly on the cheek, and then we move apart and ride sedately together down the track.

There was a long pause here then Fern heard her voice again, fainter now, as if she was running out of strength. *'I seem to be shrouded in fog, I can no longer feel the horse moving beneath me, nor can I see Rupert any more, the fog is closing in . . . What has happened, have I had a fall?*

She remained quite still hoping the throbbing in her temples would subside and wondering why she felt so utterly bereft. It had been what she requested, an enjoyable, happy experience. Instinctively she knew that the man she had met in the woods had been her lover.

Fern sat up suddenly, too suddenly, the effort made her feel nauseous and the little hammers in her head were more insistent than ever. Gritting her teeth, she swung her feet off the footrest and, with great concentration, stood up. Alex, she could see, was flushed with

235

triumph. For a moment as she looked at him she felt a shiver of fear, then, with a conscious 'pulling of herself together' she said coolly, 'I hope you are satisfied Alex, for this has been our last session. If you don't mind I am going home now.'

It took all her willpower and concentration to walk out to her car, she didn't even seek out Fiona to bid her 'goodbye'. Her legs felt as if they were made of jelly, and her hands trembled as she fitted the key into the ignition. A little distance down the road, once she was certain she was out of sight of the house, she drew into the side of the road, turned off the engine and with her arms on the steering wheel, dropped her head forward onto them. She took a deep breath—what had happened to her back there? And why had it affected her so much? She let down the window and raising her head, took another deep breath, leaning out of the window to do so. At that moment a car coming in the opposite direction drew up on the other side of the road, the driver got out and crossed over toward her. With mixed feelings she recognised Paul.

'Is anything wrong?'

Fern shook her head. 'No—no—I'm fine,' she assured him.

He looked unconvinced. 'I thought you must have broken down—or something.'

'No I just felt like—stopping—for a bit.' Fern knew even as she spoke that it sounded weak. She turned the key in the ignition. 'I'm quite okay, really.'

As she released the handbrake and applied pressure to the accelerator, he had no alternative but to step back. Fern saw him in the rear view mirror as he watched her, gave that slight Gallic shrug of his, then returned to his own car.

She drove home slowly and very carefully, wishing with all her heart that she had not given Paul the brush-off like that. His company would have been a comfort, to say the least.

Feeling completely washed out, she made herself a strong cup of tea and with it in her hand, dropped down in her most comfortable chair. There was, she decided, nothing in the world like hot strong tea at times like this. In all honesty though, she could not remember another time like this. She shivered and switched the heater on. When the shiver was repeated and she failed to warm up, she realised it had been more a prickle of fear down her spine than the cold. Just what exactly was Alex up to? She wished she knew. Hard on the heels of that thought came another, she wished Paul were here. He, perhaps, could tell her just what made Alex Cameron tick.

The knock on the door made her jump. Somehow she just knew it was Paul. She was stammering his name as she opened the door, unable to hide her pleasure and relief at seeing his large, comfortable figure framed in the doorway. She gestured for him to come in. She had wished he were here, and he was. It seemed like a minor miracle and at the same time totally right and normal.

'Tea . . . ?' she gestured at the small teapot. 'I've only just made it. I'll switch the jug back on . . .'

As she turned away, he caught hold of her arm and she had no alternative but to stand still, even to look at him. 'I was worried, you looked dreadful . . .'

'Oh, thanks!' she retorted dryly, then, meeting his eyes and seeing the genuine concern for her she added, 'Actually I felt it— but I do feel a lot better now, especially . . .' Now you are here, were the words in her mind. But all she said was, 'Tea is a great restorative.' Paul collected a mug for himself and sat down opposite her as she poured fresh boiling water onto the extra teabag she had added to the pot. She watched him as he sat silent for a moment waiting for it to brew before pouring and adding a generous helping of sugar. 'Just as I like it—hot strong and sweet, like love.' He smiled directly into her eyes as he raised the mug to his lips.

Fern lowered her lids. 'I don't usually take sugar, but I felt the need of it today,' she remarked, ignoring his remark about love.

Paul looked at her over the rim of his mug before lowering it to the table. 'Tell me,' he said at last, 'what happened, why were you so

238

upset?'

Fern was surprised at the insight that made him recognise that her malady had been of the spirit rather than the body. She took a deep breath, and then decided to tell him everything. If she couldn't trust Paul, then whom on earth could she trust, and she must talk to someone.

'It's these sessions with Alex,' she began slowly. 'I feel they are stirring up things best left alone, whether I am paying too high a price for the use of photos of his house in my book.'

'Didn't it occur to you what marvellous publicity that would be for Fiona who is at that stage in her career when she can use any boost that comes her way?'

'No—no, actually it didn't,' Fern admitted. 'I suppose that was naïve of me.'

'Somewhat,' Paul agreed, 'but I won't hold it against you. Anyway, carry on—sorry for the interruption.'

'Well—what he wanted to do was take me back in this life and beyond.'

'Beyond?'

'He believes it is possible to hypnotise a person so deeply that they go way past this life into another existence. He also thinks we access our other lives in dreams. I gather that is the main thrust of his book.'

'Do you think he led you into a past life?'

Fern nodded then shook her head. 'I don't

know. As far as I am concerned, it was a very vivid dream experience, hallucination, or whatever.'

'You could just have been accessing hidden memories of books you had read and regurgitating them as one sequence,' Paul suggested.

'I could . . .' Fern agreed, somewhat reluctantly. 'The only thing is . . .' she trailed off, suddenly embarrassed, but as he was obviously expecting more, she finally added, 'Well, I knew—the other person, very well.' Her voice dropped. 'I think, I had this feeling, I felt we were—lovers.'

'Well so far this sounds a rather pleasant experience,' Paul spoke soothingly into the silence.

Fern nodded, a slight frown on her face. 'It was all so real,' she said wistfully.

'Did you recognise any of the characters as people you know in your present life?'

She would rather not have answered this, but Paul continued to look at her waiting for her to reply, leaving her little choice but to admit the truth. 'It was you, Paul.'

She was amazed when Paul broke the tenseness with a deep belly laugh. 'I'm not very flattered meeting me, or my look alike in a hypnotic trance should cause you so much distress.'

'It wasn't seeing you, then—' Fern admitted. 'It was knowing what was to come. I had seen this man many times, in my dreams, now I knew who it was and what the connection with myself was.'

'And what was it?' Paul leaned forward slightly. 'Tell me, Fern, what was this man, this laughing cavalier of yours, what was he to you?'

'We were lovers,' she told him, in a voice devoid of expression. 'It was through me that he met his death.' Fern pushed her tea mug away and added, 'I think the feeling of guilt has been with me ever since.'

'That is absurd, I won't buy into that, and neither should you,' Paul objected.

'How safe do you really think this dabbling into other people's minds is?'

'The short answer is, I don't know.'

'And the long answer?'

'It can be very helpful. We all need to face up to issues from our past sometimes.'

'And you believe that . . . that fairy story I concocted under hypnosis was my past?' Fern demanded, quite forgetting that she had dreamed much the same story.

Paul looked down at his hands, a slight frown thawing his brows together and that unruly lock of hair that Fern always itched to push back, dropping forward, before saying quietly, 'He helped me, Fern, so I guess I thought he could maybe help you too. I'm really sorry if it hasn't worked out and I can understand you feeling I should butt out and mind my own business.'

Fern reached out and touched his arm. 'Thanks Paul, I know you meant well. I suppose if I am annoyed with anyone, it is myself.' After a moment she looked up at him directly. 'Can you share with me your experience with Alex?'

Paul hesitated, asking himself if he was ready to tell Fern, more important, if she was ready to listen. He decided to risk it and, raising the lid of the teapot. asked, 'Will this pot stand more water do you think? Confession may be good for the soul, but it can also be thirsty work.'

Fern flicked the jug on again and dropped another teabag in the pot. As she waited for the water to come to the boil, she had the feeling that somehow this was a milestone in her relationship with Paul. After topping up the pot, she sat down and waited in silence for him to speak. As she watched him pour himself more tea with a concentration that made it appear the most important thing on his mind, she wondered if he intended to say anything or had thought better of it after all.

Frowning slightly as if he were struggling to find the right words he surprised her by saying, 'You told me your dog was murdered.'

Fern nodded. 'Yes—I did say that,' she admitted, wondering why he had brought this up. He was still frowning, did he think she had used too strong a word, was that why he seemed annoyed? 'I'm sorry if you thought I was being over dramatic or shouldn't have used such an emotive word about a dog.'

'It's not for me to judge as I don't know the circumstances,' he told her. 'If that was the word you felt fitted the death of your little dog then you had every right to use it. But yes, you are right saying it is an emotive word, certainly for me.

'You see . . .' his voice was low and he took a deep breath as if psyching himself to continue, 'my daughter was murdered.'

CHAPTER ELEVEN

Fern gasped and her hand shot up to her mouth, 'Oh, my God. Paul—how dreadful. Oh, God . . .' She realised how little she knew about him, he had encouraged her to talk, but had revealed so little of himself. Now, when she met his eyes, she saw they were dark with grief he found hard to verbalise. 'What . . . how . . .?' she murmured, her own troubles momentarily lost in her feeling for his. 'Or don't you want to talk about it?'

'It was five years ago . . .' he began slowly. Five or fifty, it didn't make any difference, he thought bitterly, the pain would still be the same. His hands clenched as he thought about the man who had done it and wondered for the millionth time what sort of a creature could do that to a little girl. An animal, some said, but no animal Paul had yet met had ever done such a thing.

'Linda was abducted,' he continued after a long pause. 'Her mother, my wife, had sent her on an errand to the local store, only yards away. She went on her new bike, a two wheeler, she had it for her birthday a couple of weeks before. It was pink and still had the trainer wheels on.' What the hell did it matter what colour the bike was, he thought now, but Fern guessed he was telling her these pointless details because it delayed the moment when he had to face the real horror. 'She was just six years old, six years and two weeks.' His voice was thick with emotion. 'And this—this bastard lured her into his car somehow and took her off and raped her and strangled her.' His voice broke on a sob, 'God—I wish I could have got hold of him—I swear I would have strangled him!' He buried his face in his hands.

Fern, listening in horror, searched for the right words to say. None seemed adequate.

She leaned over and touched him very lightly with the tips of her fingers. She did not know whether he was aware for he went on, as if she had not been there.

'Pam, my wife, never got over it, she thought I blamed her . . .'

'I'm sure you didn't,' Fern said softly.

He looked up then, but almost as if he

couldn't see her. 'But I did. I said to her, *"If only you hadn't sent her to the shop"* . . . after that, I could never convince her that she was not to blame. She couldn't stand my condemnation piled on her own grief and guilt.'

For the first time in many months, Fern forgot her own pain and hurt in her absorption with that of another person. She knew all about guilt and could empathise not only with Paul but also with his wife.

'I am sure she knew—really—in her heart that you were not blaming her,' she tried to reassure him. 'She must have felt so terrible, it probably made her feel a bit better to be able to blame you for blaming her.' Fern knew what she meant, but what she was saying sounded confusing and garbled, even to herself. She could not imagine what it sounded like to Paul. 'Those dreams of mine have taught me so much about guilt, now I need to apply it in my waking life.'

With relief she saw the ghost of a smile trembling around the corners of Paul's mouth, though his eyes still glistened.

'Thank you, Fern,' he said quietly, 'for pointing that out. I should have realised that myself. I'm afraid I wasn't as much support and help to her as I should have been. But the truth was, our marriage had been a bit shaky for some time, we had even talked about separation. I guess that made us both feel guilty when this—thing—this unbelievable horror hit us . . . You read about these things in the paper and you feel real sympathy for the people involved, you try and imagine how you would feel in the same circumstances, but you can't, because you just can't believe that anything like that will ever happen to you. All the same, it was an unforgivable thing to say, and she never did forgive me.'

Fern did not know what to say. It would be pointless and utterly trite to say she was sure Paul's wife had forgiven, for obviously she had not—or why would she have left him?

Paul finally murmured, 'Sorry to have burdened you with my past sorrows, but you wanted to know how Alex helped me.'

Fern nodded. 'Tell me.'

'We met up again here by chance,' he began. 'The last time we met was at a College reunion, in New Zealand. If I was surprised to see him he was amazed to see me—here in Australia—working as a real estate agent. When I told him what had happened, why I had left New Zealand, he persuaded me to be counselled, he used light hypnosis. He didn't take the pain away, but he did make it bearable. I thought—I hoped—he could do the same for you.'

'Oh, Paul . . .' Gazing at his face, re-living old grief and pain seemed to have aged him, and at the same time made him look curiously young and very vulnerable. She reached across the table and caught his hand. 'You make me feel terrible, wallowing in self-pity, when you . . .' she broke off on a sob.

'What happened to you, Fern?' His voice was soft—and caring. 'Suppose you tell me. What *really* happened to your husband, and how does your dog fit into the story?'

Fern sifted through her painful memories, wondering where to begin. She chose the end. 'My husband killed her,' she said quietly. 'No, not accidentally. Quite deliberately—when he killed himself. He took her out with him, in the car, into the bush—and gassed himself and her.'

Paul said quietly into the ensuing silence, 'And you feel so badly because your grief for your dog seems greater than that for your husband?'

Fern gaped at him, realising in a blinding flash that what he said was true. 'But she was innocent . . . and . . . and she was more than a dog in a way, she was my surrogate child.'

She stopped aghast. How could she say this to Paul after what he had just told her? But his features remained even, his eyes beckoning her to tell him all. With grief and pain welling up in her own eyes as she remembered, she tried to explain. 'Nigel bought me Bubbles after our baby was stillborn. I said, *"Do you think a puppy can replace my baby?"* Then, her helplessness touched off my maternal instincts and I began to look after her—and love her.

She pulled me around. Then he killed her.

'Giving her to me didn't give him the right to take her away from me.' Her voice broke on a sob.

'No—it didn't,' Paul agreed. 'But he killed himself too, why?'

Fern looked at him through swimming eyes. 'Because I wasn't there, and he was jealous of her, thought I loved her too much—he knew how much it would hurt me. I was away, in Tassie, I had to go—Gran was dying. Even though I could see he was going into one of his dark moods, I told myself he would be all right, even though I could see he was heading downhill.' She paused, and took a great gulping breath. 'I owed Gran so much, she took me in when my parents died and gave me a truly wonderful childhood, I had to go.'

'Of course you did,' Paul said gently. 'Was your husband a manic depressive, did he suffer from what they now call Bi-Polar disorder?'

The way he spoke reminded Fern suddenly of something he had said earlier. She turned her tear-drenched face towards him. 'You said you were at college with Alex, what did you study?' She was momentarily deflected.

'Psychology,' he said briefly. 'Was he being treated?'

She shook her head. 'He refused to admit there was anything wrong, but we lived life on the roller coaster of his mood swings. But if you studied psychology why . . .'

'Am I a real estate agent and not a practicing shrink?' There was a bitter note in his voice. 'I gave it up after—after Pam left. If I couldn't even help my own wife when she needed it, then what use was I?'

'Oh, Paul . . .' She wanted to tell him not to be so hard on himself, that his own experiences gave him a greater understanding for others—but he, not her, was the psychologist.

When he noticed the time and with the excuse that he was already late for an appointment with an important client, Fern wondered if he was sorry he had told her so much.

She wanted him to stay, to comfort and be comforted and briefly she saw the same need in his eyes, felt it in his touch as he kissed her swiftly. 'I'm sorry . . .' he told her, 'I really do have to go.'

The door closed and she felt suddenly alone in her cottage, usually so calm and comforting. Restless on her own, nothing could hold her attention, she tried her laptop, television, a book, but always her thoughts turned back to Paul. She thought of his appalling tragedy and wondered how long it took to get over a loss like that. Or if, indeed, one ever did. She worried that he would think her story nothing compared to his own and that he would think her selfish and self-centred.

She soon convinced herself that she would

never see him again.

She forced herself to fire up her laptop. Wasn't work the great antidote to all emotional problems? 'Hold on, Fern Barclay . . .' she admonished herself out loud. 'What emotional problems?' Her whole aim in coming here had been to leave those behind. To start life afresh with a clean slate. She had succeeded, hadn't she?

Then why did she feel as if a leaden ball had replaced her heart when she thought she might never see Paul again?

CHAPTER TWELVE

In a determined effort to lose herself in work Fern turned back to her laptop, pulling her colour charts and swatches around her, but she found it hard to concentrate. She pushed them to one side and started going through the files of her own writing on her computer with a view to selecting some for the book she was endeavouring to put together. But however hard she tried to keep him out, Paul seemed to manage to worm his way into her thoughts.

This, she told herself, is ridiculous. I am behaving like a lovesick schoolgirl instead of a mature widow. Just saying that word to herself pulled her up short. Curious, but she had never before thought of herself as a widow.

The very word conjured up for her a picture of an aging, fading female draped in trailing black, the proverbial 'widow's weeds'. That was not at all how she wanted to see herself, or to be seen by others. Since she had left Melbourne and started her new life here, she had endeavoured to build up a picture of herself as independent, self-contained, the very epitome of the successful career woman on her own. Now that vision was beginning to tarnish and she wasn't even sure she was capable of burnishing it up again, or even if she wanted to.

Abandoning all pretence of work, she got up and walked over to the window. Where was Paul now—and why had he really left so suddenly? Had she said something to upset him? She didn't think so, but then—it was often so hard to tell what would offend a person. With an effort of will, she turned her attention back to her computer. It seemed that all this agonising was purely academic. Sure Paul had confided in her the story of the tragedy that darkened his own life, but it seemed to her, the more she thought about it, that the telling had been an obscure way of saying to her 'back off—I've done with emotional entanglements'. She could respect that, even accept it, for wasn't that the same message she had been giving him all these weeks?

She had just got her thoughts more or less

under control when the phone rang. It was Paul. and immediately all her carefully martialled good sense faded away.

'Look . . .' he was saying, 'I'm sorry I dashed off like that.'

'That's okay . . .' Fern answered graciously. 'I understand. Don't give it a thought. I haven't.' Childishly, she crossed her fingers as she told the lie. 'I've been too busy.'

'Oh—Oh—well that's all right then. I was going to—but if you are busy . . .' He trailed off leaving so much unsaid.

'Oh—I've finished now,' Fern cut in swiftly.

'In that case—I wondered if you would meet me for dinner—or . . .'

'Or you could come here,' Fern supplied. 'I'll cook for you.' Suddenly she wanted to do something for him, to care for him, it was a long time since she had felt like this about anyone.

Fern slowly replaced the phone. It was as if, in saying those last four words, which had slipped out without thinking, she had moved their relationship into a totally different sphere.

After a good deal of thought, she decided on simplicity and the meal she offered him was steak and salads.

'This is good.' He helped himself to another serving of watermelon salad as he spoke, 'I don't think I've ever had watermelon served like this before.' He turned pieces over on his plate looking at it carefully. 'Watermelon, onion and mint, is that it?'

'That's it. It was one of Gran's specialities.'

'You often talk about your grandmother.' He remembered hearing her trot out those trite, but oh, so true, sayings beloved of an earlier generation. 'She meant a lot to you, I feel.' His voice was gentle.

'Yes—a great deal, more I suppose than most grandmothers. When my father died, she sent for us, my mother and I, to go home—to her—in Tassie. I was three years old at the time, we had only been there about six months, maybe a little longer, I can't really remember, when my mother left, with a new man.' She paused, silent for so long, that Paul asked,

'Did you ever see her again?'

'No—she was killed in a road accident in Queensland. I haven't any very clear memories of either of my parents, just Gran.' She smiled suddenly as happy memories flooded back, 'I adored her and loved the farm, I never wanted to leave it.'

'But you did . . .' he prompted gently, watching a shadow cross her face.

'I met Nigel.' Her voice was terse. She got up and began fiddling around, collecting almond slices she had bought as a dessert and putting coffee in the plunger.

He waited in silence until she sat down. 'Nigel?' he made a question of the name and when she still did not speak added, 'Your

253

husband?'

Fern nodded. 'My late husband,' she corrected. Her words fell into a well of silence.

Paul waited, his gut feeling told him that if he wanted to hear more, he must not push her. His instinct was correct, hard as it was to talk Fern found the silence even more unbearable.

She spoke tonelessly, but when she looked up, Paul was startled at the anger blazing through the hurt in her eyes. After a pause, she continued in the same flat voice, speaking her thoughts out loud. 'I should have listened to Gran in the first place, she begged me to wait, we had only known one another six weeks when we were married. With the wisdom of hindsight, I realise Nigel was in his manic phase, full of frenetic energy and wild enthusiasm. He carried me along with it. If I had listened to Gran and waited, I would have seen the other side to him.' She paused and thought for a moment before adding truthfully, 'But I don't suppose it would have made any difference.'

'No,' he agreed, 'I don't suppose it would. People in love are not noted for listening to reason.'

'I was in love all right, and idealistic and romantic—and very young.' She was silent again for a few moments, letting her thoughts slide back over the years of her marriage. 'Can you believe it—I truly thought for the first few years that I was the one to blame, that I did something to upset him. His first suicide attempt was when I was pregnant. They pumped him out then and saved him. Shortly after I went into premature labour. I blamed him for the baby dying. Unfair of me I know.'

'But understandable,' he said gently. What a story, everyone she had mentioned was dead, he wondered if she had anyone in the world to call her own.

'But I also felt guilty,' she went on as if he hadn't spoken. 'Especially when he did kill himself.'

'The nearest and dearest of suicides usually do,' Paul pointed out.

'What a wallow in self-pity!' With a wry expression Fern jumped to her feet abruptly and crossed the room to make the coffee. 'Sorry . . .' she apologised as she brought it to the table. 'And now, just to make sure I continue to feel guilty about something, I feel responsible for your death.' Her grin was rather lop-sided, was she actually admitting to a belief in his ideas?

'My death?' For a moment he was nonplussed. 'But I am alive—I think!' He pinched his arm and smiled at her. 'Or are you talking about three hundred years ago?'

'If my dreams, both sleeping and under Alex's powers of hypnosis, are to be believed.' She had herself in hand now and managed to sound both cool and slightly scornful. 'What a good thing I don't agree with your ideas about

255

reincarnation, or I would have to worry about you.'

In spite of her carefully controlled little speech and the implication that what happened to him was of no concern to her, Paul was sure she was deliberately raising a barrier between them, he knew that he must break it down or he risked losing her for ever. This realisation brought with it the sudden conviction that he couldn't bear that. He reached across the table and took her hand in his.

'Fern—will you trust me and try an experiment?'

'If you are suggesting another session with Alex the answer is a definite no.'

He shook his head. 'No, not with Alex, with me. But you must trust me.'

'As a psychologist—or as a man?' She wished she could control the absurd wobble in her voice.

'Will you let me hypnotise you?' His voice was soft and persuasive. He felt sure that if he could take her back to a time when they had been happy together he could achieve two things, break the cycle of her distressing dreams and satisfy his own curiosity about where he had known her. But first he knew he had to rid her of some of her load of guilt.

He stood up, and holding her hand led her gently over to the big armchair. Wordlessly, she sat down.

He began to talk, softly, gently, and almost monotonously emphasising she was not to hold herself responsible for the things that had happened. 'We are each,' he told her, 'in charge of our own lives. What Nigel did, he did because of something in himself, not because of anything you did, or failed to do. 'As he talked, he felt, in a curious way, his own load of guilt sliding off his back. Then slowly, he took her back—back—it was as if she was going down a long dark tunnel, then his voice telling her; 'Now, think of me, Paul, I am thinking of you, Fern. Try and remember a time when you and I were together and completely happy. I am also remembering . . .'

It was a warm Spring day, her heightened senses made her aware of the feel of the sun, the sound of the birds, the very scent of Spring, even the vibration of the ground beneath her. Then she realised that it was vibrating because a horseman was riding towards her. She looked up, it was him, she caught her breath in a gasp of delight before breaking into a run. She reached the horse as he slid to the ground and caught her up in his arms. 'You are home!' she cried. As he held her close and looked deep into her eyes, she was aware of the most pure and perfect happiness.

Feeling the transience of the moment she returned to the present. Paul was sitting opposite her, apparently asleep. Not alert and in control of the situation as she had been used to finding Alex when she 'came to' after one of their sessions.

He opened his eyes and looking into her face, still glowing from the joy of their reunion, he knew they had both returned from a meeting in another time zone.

It had worked, he couldn't believe it—but—it had worked! He reached for her hands, drawing her close and smiling into her eyes in a way that made her senses throb.

'I was riding home, the sun was shining, it was a beautiful Spring day, you were running to meet me. In that exquisite moment we were perfectly happy, weren't we?'

Fern nodded in amazement—he was describing what she had experienced—perhaps—maybe . . .

Silently she led him to the bedroom, or he led her, she couldn't be sure. Nor could she be entirely sure if this were really happening or if she were still in a dream. They undressed each other with the unhurried ease of two people who have known one another for a long time and have every hope of being together for a great deal more.

With one hand on either side of his head she pulled his face towards hers, groaning slightly with pure delight as his tongue slid between her parted lips. There was no need to snatch at the tatters of her pride and independence, for as he caressed with a gentle kiss, first one nipple, then the other and her body arched towards him, she knew that they met as equals. That was how it had always been, and always would be, their love was timeless, as was their need for each other. As he slid into her, she held his body close—as close as she could—wrapping her legs as well as her arms around him, and in the searing moment when they climaxed together, she felt that not only their bodies but their souls fused into one in that perfect moment of union.

Afterwards as they lay together, she ran a finger down his body, softly tracing the line of his sternum.

'I think,' she murmured, 'that such a good psychologist is wasted on the world of real estate?'

'So Alex suggested, but then he had an ulterior motive. He wants me to take over his practice for six months while he concentrates on writing his book. I've been thinking about it for a while, but hadn't made up my mind. That's why I went to Melbourne, to see what the future holds instead of thinking about the past for a change.'

'And . . .'

'It would mean living in Melbourne— leaving you,' he murmured drowsily against her hair.

Fern wondered how to express her feelings without capitulating completely to an acceptance of Paul's ideas. 'I won't sell the cottage, or even lease it, we can come up here for weekends, holidays, maybe for ever when you have done your six month stint.' After a while she added softly, 'I found healing—and you—in it. Not to mention a cat who seems to have always lived here.' She smiled as she said that.

But Paul answered seriously, 'Perhaps he has—perhaps we all have. Lying here with you, completely relaxed, staring at that wallpaper, I suddenly knew just why it seemed so familiar.'

'I suppose you are going to say we lived in this house when the original paper was fresh ...' Her voice faded and lost its teasing note as she remembered her dream of farewelling a First World War soldier. 'Perhaps . . .' she found herself murmuring against his heart.

Fern could feel drowsiness taking over, but there were things to settle. 'You do the six months for Alex, we owe him that, after all he helped me find you, and I will write my book, maybe after that we will come back—for ever.'

He laughed and drew her even closer. 'Oh, my darling, you haven't changed one bit, from your red hair to your organising ability.'

She was about to remind him that she didn't share his belief in many lives, but as she lay secure in his arms, she knew she would like to, if she could spend them all with him.

We hope you have enjoyed this Large Print book. Other Chivers Press or Thorndike Press Large Print books are available at your library or directly from the publishers.

For more information about current and forthcoming titles, please call or write, without obligation, to:

Chivers Large Print
published by BBC Audiobooks Ltd
St James House, The Square
Lower Bristol Road
Bath BA2 3BH
UK
email: bbcaudiobooks@bbc.co.uk
www.bbcaudiobooks.co.uk

OR

Thorndike Press
295 Kennedy Memorial Drive
Waterville
Maine 04901
USA
www.gale.com/thorndike
www.gale.com/wheeler

All our Large Print titles are designed for easy reading, and all our books are made to last.